Past And Future Lives In China

Love And Death In China: Book Two
The Sequel To "The Way Of The Dragon"

Martin Avery

Dedication: To the people I've met in past and future lives.

ISBN # 978-1-312-39704-0   .

To dwell in the here and now does not mean you never think about the past, or responsibly plan for the future. The idea is simply not to allow yourself to get lost in regrets about the past or worries about the future. If you are firmly grounded in the present moment, the past can be an object of inquiry, the object of your mindfulness and concentration. You can attain many insights by looking into the past, but you are still grounded in the present moment. ~ Thich Nhat Hanh

"If you're lost you can look - and you will find me
Time after time
If you fall I will catch you - I'll be waiting
Time after time ...."
~ from "Time After Time", writers: Marco Pirroni, Marcel Jacob, Cyndi Lauper, Nathan Tyrone Payton, Rob Hyman, Adam Ant, Jeff Scott Soto, Robert Hyman

Past And Future Lives In China

Love And Death In China: Book Two
The Sequel To "The Way Of The Dragon"

Martin Avery

Javier: What are you reading?
Luisa Rey: Old letters.
Javier: Why do you keep reading them?
Luisa Rey: I don't know. Just trying to understand something.
Javier: What?
Luisa Rey: Why we keep making the same mistakes... over and over.
~ from Cloud Atlas, a 2012 epic adventure drama film adapted from the 2004 novel of the same name by David Mitchell

"Love the world and yourself in it, move through it as though it offers no resistance, as though the world is your natural element."
— Audrey Niffenegger, The Time Traveler's Wife

When I say the magic word to all these people, they will vanish forever. I will then say the magic words to you, and you, too, will vanish -- never to be seen again.
-- Kurt Vonnegut Jr., "Between Time and Timbuktu"

People aren't supposed to look back. I'm certainly not going to do it anymore. I've finished my war book now. The next one I write is going to be fun. This one is a failure, and had to be, since it was written by a pillar of salt. It begins like this: "Listen: Billy Pilgrim has come unstuck in time." — from Slaughterhouse-Five, Or The Children's Crusade : A Duty-dance with Death, by Kurt Vonnegut.

I believe that I was a dog in a past life. That's the only thing that would explain why I like to snack on Purina Dog Chow.
— Dean Koontz

You know, I think I had my first past life recall when I was 7.
— Shirley MacLaine

"I recognized you instantly. All of our lives flashed through my mind in a split second. I felt a pull so strongly towards you that I almost couldn't stop it."
— J. Sterling, In Dreams

"I live my life until I start the cycle of my dreams,then I leave and search for you until I die.When I come back, I live to remember, I live to find you"
— Molly Bryant, Wandering Souls

"No matter how you arrive at the awareness and belief that you've lived before and will live again, the most lasting healing benefit will be the change in your attitude. You are creating your future lives right at this moment, and every moment of decision-making."

— Lianne Downey, Speed Your Evolution: Become the Star Being You Are Meant to Be

"If the stock market exists, so must previous lives."
— Margaret Atwood, Good Bones and Simple Murders

"When the incarnation of the Dakini marked by the dragon is found by her mirror, the chains of the dragon will melt from the land of snows."
— Daniel Prokop, Taking It with You

"Every single thing you do, and everything that is done for you, is attached to at least a thousand other threads. Don't ever think any action is operating in your orbit independent of the rest of your life." Carolyn Myss

"Just let go. Let go of how you thought your life should be, and embrace the life that is trying to work its way into your consciousness." Caroline Myss

"The "Key of Heaven" is a video game developed by Climax. It is an action RPG (role playing game) with a distinctly Oriental flavour. You take the role of Shinbu, a former disciple of the Seiryu clan, who got kicked out of his community for attempting to read what was written on the 'Monument of Secrets'. What was written there was the key to heaven. It is something only the hardest of the hard are permitted to do.

I won't reveal the secret of the game but I can give you this hint: It has something to do with using healing medicine as soon as you get tired.

I studied with Margot Anand after reading her book, Everyday Ecstasy, which reveals the seven Tantric keys to heaven. They are called The Root of Creation, The Flowing Stream, The Radiant Sun, The Pulse of Life, The Song of the Soul, The Full Moon, and The Open Sky.

Those keys are the names of meditative exercises aimed at clearing and then filling the seven main chakras. Anand recommends doing the exercises first thing in the morning to create a joyous, harmonious day.

I studied with Deepak Chopra after reading his books, Seven Spiritual Laws of Success and The Book of Secrets: Unlocking the Hidden Dimensions of Your Life. He suggests these three keys will let you in to heaven: 1. Don't make this a self-improvement project. 2. Don't set yourself a timetable. And 3. Don't wait for a miracle.

Louise L. Hayes, on the other hand, says, "This Earth is our heaven."

I studied with Janet Amare after reading her book, Soul Purpose. She teaches a course in energy medicine leading to a Certificate In Spiritual Healing (CISH) for the Centre of International Holistic Studies, located in Toronto. She taught us how to do Past Life work, and many other things." -- from The Keys To Heaven, by Martin Avery, in Timeless Spirit

Magazines

Table Of Contents

Prologue: Past Life Work

Do you have a sense of your past lives? Perhaps you feel drawn to one time or another in earth's history? Or perhaps to the stories of Atlantis and Lemuria, to ancient civilizations or, indeed, to notions of lives on other planets? Or perhaps you are really just curious about who and what you WERE and how that impacts on who you are now?

There are websites that will welcome you and your wallet!

Discovery of our past-life stories can be useful tools in understanding ourselves.

And so, if you are yearning to find out more about yourself, then I am willing and able to facilitate that!

That's the kind of things they say online!

Here's the past life test:

Is your soul talking to you about your past lives? More importantly, are you listening? These 25 questions help you find out.

1. Have you ever had a dream where you woke up, and it felt so real that it took you a while to 'come back' to your life?

2. Do you have an interest or talent, that was very different from your family of origin?

3. For the purpose of this past life test, have you attracted the same kind of partner again and again?

4. Are you a collector? Why do you think you were you drawn to your particular passion?

5. Have you ever felt 'dread' when you met someone, yet were compelled to get closer to them?

6. Have you ever been irrationally scared to lose someone in an accident (for example), even when you don't have a logical reason to be scared?

7. Have you ever done something completely out of character because of meeting someone?

8. Have you ever watched a movie or TV show, and began to cry at a particular story line? What character did you relate to most?

9. Have you ever been strongly drawn to a particular place, or a time in history?

10. Have you ever had a strong connection with (or fear of) a particular animal?

11. For the purpose of this past life test, did you have any unusual childhood experiences?

12. Do you have irrational fears or phobias about something or someone, that has no logical connection to this life?

13. Have you ever had obsessive feelings about someone or something, especially if you're generally a logical person?

14. Have you ever taken a wrong turn, which lead to the unexpected?

15. Have you ever had deep emotions about something or someone, without a reason?

16. Have you ever had an experience that was so 'strange' that you couldn't explain it?

17. Have you ever met someone, and been irresistibly drawn to them, a if there was something pulling you together?

18. Have you ever been relaxed, when an image popped into your mind: a face you 'knew' but didn't recognize?

19. For the purpose of this past life test, have you ever been strongly attracted or repulsed by someone you just met for no logical reason?

20. Have you ever overheard a conversation that came at exactly the right time for you?

21. Have you ever heard a 'voice' in your head say something that you had never considered before?

22. Have you ever encountered the same story-theme again and again (say in movies or books), by coincidence?

23. Have you ever experienced déjà vu?

24. Have you ever had a natural talent for something that you had no training in?

25. Have you ever had someone say particular words, that stood out? Then did you hear these words again (maybe from someone else)?

I have a certificate in Past Life Work. It was part of the course work for my Diploma In Spiritual Healing from the College of International Holistic Studies, in Canada. They have a fascinating place not far from Hamilton, in southern Ontario.

I will reveal all my secrets and describe how it's done.

First, you get your client to relax. You use the mildest form of hypnosis. You speak in a calm voice, using healing chi.

Did you know you can heal with your voice chi?

It's all about energy!

Your client, or patient, relaxes into a meditative state and you lead them on a guided meditation, coaching them to visual a series of suggested images, and then they have a vivid vision like a dream. You bring them back into the here and now and encourage them to write down what they experienced, so the information isn't lost.

The series of images you guide them to see can vary. If you are working with someone athletic, you might take them to a ski lift, in their minds, or a beach.

The beach works best for many people.

Have them picture their favourite beach in the world and ask them to imagine being there on the perfect day. Coach them to feel the sand, the water, the air, and tell them to make it just the way they like it.

The first change you introduce to the scenario that is so familiar to them is an extension. Tell them to imagine and visualize their beach in a slightly different way.

When you look up the beach and down the beach, you notice that it is longer than before. It is much longer. The beach stretches to the horizon in both directions. It appears to stretch beyond both horizons.

I like to make use of JinShiTan beach, or Golden Pebble Beach, near JinShiTan Station, which is part of Dalian, in China. It's a beautiful beach on the Yellow Sea with a long curving section that has the Black Mountains as a backdrop. The beach is decorated beautifully with a bridge called the Golden Bay Bridge.

I imagine that Golden Bay and Golden Pebble Beach goes on forever, not just the length of China and Asia but far, far beyond.

To get you ready for traveling in time, it can be useful to think about time, a bit, and your idea of time, and your sense of world history.

Not everyone can be a world history master, especially when we tend to learn about it in specifically segmented classes like "European History". Maybe you have an exceptional grasp on the global historical timeline. But for those of us who don't, the list below, inspired by a recent Reddit thread called "What are two events that took place in the same time in history but don't seem like they would have?" puts key historical moments into some much-needed context.

1. Betty White is older than sliced bread, which was introduced in 1928. Before that, bread was sold in whole loaves as bakers didn't trust sliced bread could stay fresh. Betty White was born in 1922 and spent her early years not eating sliced bread. But White recently celebrated her 92nd birthday, which means she's been able to experience the first "greatest invention" much longer than most of us.

2. Harvard University was founded before calculus was invented.

Established in 1636, Harvard is the oldest institution of higher education in the U.S. The "New College," as it was originally called, had no calculus classes because it didn't exist yet. The invention of calculus would come in the late 17th century with Gottfried Leibniz's 1684 publication of "Nova Methodus," and in part with Isaac Newton's"Principia" in 1687, followed by additional explanations and reformulations by subsequent mathematicians. Also, European physicist, mathematician and astronomer Galileo was still alive during Harvard's early years -- he died in 1642.

3. The last time the Chicago Cubs won a World Series, the Ottoman Empire still existed.

The Chicago Cubs haven't won a World Series since 1908. This was back when there were still teams such as the Brooklyn Superbs and the Boston Doves. The Ottoman

Empire, which was founded in the 13th century, also existed back then. Mehmed VI was the last sultan of the empire and his reign ended in 1922 when the sultanate was abolished and the Turkish government took governing control over the new republic -- 14 years after the Cubs last won the World Series.

Let's not even mention the Toronto Maple Leafs!

The last time they won the Stanley Cup, I still lived in Norman Bethune's hometown, played for the peewee all-star hockey team, and danced with a group of Grade 7 kids in our school's celebration for Canada's centennial!

4. The Pyramids of Giza were built in the time of wooly mammoths.

From what we can tell, the last of the wooly mammoth died out around 1700 B.C. on Russia's Wrangel Island. In Egypt, the Pyramids of Giza were built around 4,000 years ago, although there have been claims that they're even older. This also means that Cleopatra's time on Earth is actually closer to us in history than to the construction of the pyramids.

5. The fax machine was invented the same year as the Oregon trail migration.

The first fax machine was invented in 1843 by a Scottish mechanic named Alexander Bain. This early model used a combination of synchronized pendulums, electric probes and electrochemically sensitive paper to scan documents, and then send the information over a series of wires to be reproduced. The "Great Migration" on the Oregon trail began the same year, when a wagon train of about 1,000 migrants attempted to travel west, but probably died of dysentery along the way.

6. The jewelry store Tiffany & Co. was founded before Italy was a country.

While Rome was officially a holdout for a number of years after, in 1861 General Giuseppe Garibaldi led a successful campaign to gather the various city-states and bring them under one nation. Charles Lewis Tiffany and John B. Young founded Tiffany & Young in 1837 and then became Tiffany & Co. in 1853. This means Audrey Hepburn could have gotten "breakfast at Tiffany's" before she could have had her Italian "Roman Holiday.

7. France was still using the guillotine when "Star Wars" came out.

The last time the guillotine was used as a form of execution in France was in 1977. The guillotine lasted for about two centuries. The first "Star Wars" film was also released in 1977 a few months before the execution.

Another mind-blowing historical fact from France: The Eiffel Tower was completed in 1889, which is the same year Nintendo was founded and that Van Gogh painted "The Starry Night."

Chapter 1: Past Life #1: With Dr. Henry Norman Bethune In China

Doing Past Life work is something I find fascinating, as well as healing, and I've discovered that it gets easier and easier to do, the more you do it, but it can be a bit of a problem when the past intrudes on the present. It's good to have an awareness of your past lives, and what you can learn from them, but you don't want to wander around in the past all the time. It's important to live in the moment, as they say, or stay in the here and now.

I've read a lot of science fiction novels and seen many sci-fi movies about time travel, including a number of stories about people who get lots in time or un-stuck or whose multiple lives colliding at different times cause problems. The movie called The Time-Traveller's Wife comes immediately to mind, along with Between Time and Timbuktu by Kurt Vonnegut.

Generally, the past stays in the past, for me, but I have to say that while I am here in China, it does not take much to make me feel as though I am back in Bethune's time.

I've written a book about that.

The energy you feel in China is quite grounding, generally, unlike the energy of, for instance, India or Nepal, which make you feel as though you are barely connected to the planet Earth and might fly off at any time. Even so, in China I feel as though I can easily go back in time to the years when Bethune was here.

Instead of meditating and doing guided visualizations to hook up with a guide on a never-ending beach, the way I usually to past life work, all it takes for me to travel back to Bethune's time is a few minutes with nothing to do. As a song from the Sixties said, all I have to do is dream. And the problem is, gee whiz, I don't want to dream my life away.

If I'm early for a meeting, or others are late, and I have a few minutes to myself, or while I enjoy my quick commute to work, which is a five minute walk, or when I'm waiting for a train or riding one, or while I'm waiting in a restaurant for lunch to arrive, I think about Bethune for a second and I am gone .... Lost in time.

Like Roderick and Sharon Stewart, I've spent decades tracking down information about Bethune's life in Canada, starting in our hometown, and his work in Spain during the civil war, fighting fascism, as well as his service as a guerrilla doctor to communist forces in China.

I have read everything by and about Bethune and interviewed some people who knew him.

Their book about Bethune called Phoenix: The Life of Norman Bethune, is quite thorough but it's not exactly objective, in my opinion, as it paints a picture of this heroic figure, this international humanitarian, as a very 'human' being.

The son of a Presbyterian minister, Bethune alienated a number of his colleagues, friends, and various women he pursued.

The Stewarts speculated that Bethune had a borderline personality disorder, say he was clearly an alcoholic and may have abused morphine, lied about his communism, defrauded an insurance company, and carried out abortions. They say a Western doctor who knew him best in China considered him "psychopathic" and "a horrible man," the Canadian communists who funded Bethune's medical work in Spain were appalled by his wild drinking and spending and his inability to get along with the Spaniards.

They say he realized that he had no future in medicine in Canada, and that was why Bethune went to China in 1938: to seek redemption as a good communist doctor in the war against Japan.

I don't know about any of that.

When I go back in time, it is not to Spain or Canada. I have never seen Bethune anywhere except in China. And what I have seen of Beth in China is the time the Stewarts describe him rising, phoenix-like, to several months' of high levels of sacrifice and service tending to wounded soldiers of Mao Zedong's Eighth Route Army before dying of the effects of septicemia.

In China, Bethune worked long hours and saved thousands of lives, but the American and Canadian communist organizations that financed his mission gave him no ongoing support, ignoring his pleas for money and supplies.

Bethune's fame is largely the result of the fact that the side he was fighting for won. The ultimate victory of the Chinese over the Japanese, and the Chinese communists over the Guodmindang in the Chinese civil war, right after the war with Japan, assured Bethune a place in history.

His deeds were immortalized for political purposes, first by the government of China during the Great Proletarian Cultural Revolution of the 1960s, then by the government of Canada in the 1970s as it tried to develop relations with the government of China and with the Chinese people. The campaign to celebrate Bethune largely succeeded.

Bethune's moment of success compares to the achievements of countless physicians, from country practitioners and laboratory researchers through skilled surgeons through the thousands of Christian medical missionaries who first brought Western medicine to China. Bethune achieved a kind of glamorous battlefield humanitarianism and a degree of personal satisfaction.

Even the worst doctor usually does some good in this suffering world.

Bethune died with his boots on, became a martyr fighting for the good of the cause he believed in, and is still recognized as an international hero. He remains a famous figure in Spain, Canada, and China to this day.

When I travel back in time to the days when Bethune was living and working in China, I am always the same person: a Chinese doctor of Traditional Chinese Medicine, conscripted by Bethune for a crash course in Western medicine, so I could assist him as a guerrilla surgeon saving lives right by the front lines in the battle.

When I close my eyes, I can see him working in the worst conditions, saving lives, doing surgery for seventy-two hours at a stretch, without sleep, eating as he worked, getting energy from who knows where except grace.

He aged quickly, while he was working as a wartime surgeon in Canada; you could actually see him getting older day after day after day. He did nothing to preserve his own health: he did not take breaks, get exercise, take time to eat or sleep, or look after any of his needs, from nutrition to mental health. He just worked and worked like a man obsessed with surgery and with saving lives.

If he wasn't cutting or stitching, trying to save another life, he was writing a manual for me, and the others he wanted to train to work alongside of him and after he was gone. He gave us the books he wrote and taught us, quickly, while he worked, showing us how to cut, how to stitch, how to work with blood, and he was interested in what we knew, as Chinese medicine was quite different, but he never took any time to talk to us about it or learn anything about it.

"There's no time for that, now," he said. "Maybe you can help them heal after I get them patched up."

That was it.

When I go back to Bethune's time, I learn little of my own life as I was mesmerized by him and the work he did while the battled raged all around us.

6. A Woman With The Eighth Route Army

When he regained consciousness, as Bobby Clobber used to say on Air Farce, he wanted to get right back at it.

"There's someone I want you to meet," he said. "Let's go back in time, to that same time, but just a little bit earlier."

"Who?" I asked.

"A woman," he said.

"A woman with the Eighth Route Army?" I said. "That's incredible!"

"I know!" Bethune said.

"Did you ...."

"Fall in love with her?" he finished the sentence for me. "No, it wasn't like that. -- She was something else."

"Who?" I asked.

"Agnes Smedley," he said.

"Who?" I said again.

"You sound like an owl," Bethune said. "Who? Who?"

"Well, who was she?" I said.

"Agnes Smedley recruited me," he said.

It is difficult to convey in a few brief words how a working-class woman, born in northern Missouri of an itinerant miner and a boarding house cook and raised in the Rockefeller 'mining camps' where the Colorado Fuel and Iron Company owned 'everything but the air,' and who never even finished grade school came to write: 'I have but one loyalty, one faith, and that was to the liberation of the poor and oppressed; and within that framework, to the Chinese Revolution as it has now materialized'," Bethune said.

"However it is possible to indicate something of the experiences which led her to this declaration."

He went on to tell me her life story:

After working for several years at all sorts of unskilled labour, from tobacco stripper, stenographer, waitress, book agent or 'just plain starveling', married and quickly divorced, she left the Southwest in her early twenties for New York City. There her arrest and solitary confinement in the Tombs in 1918 (she had worked as a 'sort of communications centre' for Indian Nationalists in New York) as an alleged 'German agent' merely served to cement her early hatred for the capitalist system.

Late in 1919, the charges finally dismissed, she boarded a freighter bound for Europe. In Berlin, looking for the newspaper of the Indian exiles on whose behalf she had been imprisoned, she met the revolutionary leader Virendranath Chattopadhyaya. She lived with him eight years, studying Indian history and Chinese nationalism. In Berlin, she and a group of progressive physicians with some financial aid from Margaret Sanger set up the first state birth-control clinic. The German republican government took the clinic over and established several others which flourished until the Nazis came to power and women were 'ordered back to the bedroom'. With Hitler threatening, Viren left Germany for the Academy of Sciences in Leningrad, and Agnes obtained a position with the Frankfurter Zeitung in 1928 as a special correspondent in China.

Entering China from the Soviet-Chinese frontier at Manchouli, Agnes felt she had just entered the Middle Ages. She decided at that time that: 'Live apart from the Chinese people I would not. The road to an understanding of them and their country led only into their ranks; nor did there seem any other way for me to justify my existence among them.'

In Manchuria she soon realised 'the extent of Japanese economic control and political power over railways, government machinery, investments in factories and land'. Her first series of articles on Japan's Mailed Fist in Manchuria were not published until Japan actually invaded Manchuria September 18, 1931.

The foreign press as well as the Chinese press had been either bought off or silenced. Agnes learned of contracts between Reuters, official British News Agency, and the KMT whereby the Agency received 10,000 dollars a month in exchange for 'favourable publicity' to the KMT government. Similar contracts with American agencies were common knowledge. While the foreign press reported on the 'progress' made by the KMT government between the Great Revolution of 1929 up to the China-Japanese War of 1937-45, Agnes reported about places where prisoners, even anti-communists and nationalists, were publicly beheaded for being trade unionists, coolie league organisers or intellectuals. Because of her work the British Secret Service claimed that she was a British subject married to an Indian seditionist and travelling with a 'false' passport. It was only with great effort that the American Consul was reminded that they owed duty to their citizens somewhat higher than that to the British Foreign Office.

Making Shanghai her headquarters, Agnes exposed the corrupt, collusive, treasonous activities of the KMT officials who openly collaborated with the Japanese in Manchuria. She found that the KMT had only 39,000 members out of a population of 450 million, and that it 'had become, in other words, a small closed corporation of government officials and their subordinates.' Trade union fees were merely tributes to the KMT used to ensure that no organizing occurred; agrarian reforms were non-existent.

In 1930 Agnes met Lu Xun, the great Chinese writer, 'the man who became one of the most influential factors in my life during all my years in China.' Together with other intellectuals in mid-1932 they formed the first 'League of Civil Rights' in China to urge democratic rights and an end to the torturing and massacre of political prisoners.

In 1932 the Frankfurter Zeitung, now dominated by the Nazis, fired Agnes. With no money or job her health began to fail and in 1933 she went to Russia to recuperate for eleven months and there finished her book 'China's Red Army Marches'. However, she 'could not imagine spending [her] life outside China,' and made plans to return to China via the US where she hoped to establish herself as correspondent for some publication. No paper dared hire her and she yearned to leave that 'strange planet' America, as soon as possible.

By spring 1936 she was in Shangand, far from well Agnes was advised to go to Xian to recuperate. Thus she was afforded first hand experience of the capture of Chiang Kaishek, by soldiers infuriated by Nanjing's 'surrender policy'. (Japan, up to that point, had occupied Manchuria and a large area of north China and his armies were being ordered to fight 'communists' rather than the Japanese invaders.) Shortly afterwards, Agnes left for the Red Army headquarters in Yan'an where she met for the first time Mao Zedong and Zhou Enlai and later Lin Biao. After meeting Zhu De, Commander-in-Chief of the Red Army, she undertook to write his biography but was interrupted when the Japanese launched a full scale invasion into China immediately after the Luguoqiao Incident, 7 July 1937.

Agnes joined the Red Army (renamed the Eighth Route Army after Chiang was finally forced to enter into the United Front with the Communists). By September, 1937 Agnes was on her way to Suiyuan and Chahar provinces where the Red Army was fighting. Although in constant pain from back injury, she reported about the condition of the wounded, about the starvation and rampant disease; and appealed for medical aid seeing the absolute necessity for 'travelling dispensaries and public health workers'. She soon became a sort of 'wandering first aid worker' herself, often treating soldiers from her stretcher when she could no longer sit or stand. Impressed by marching with that Workers' and Peasants' Army, seeing its success in mobilising the peasants into 'partisan warfare' and witnessing the moral conviction of its soldiers who bravely resisted the Japanese, Agnes became: '. . . irrevocably convinced that the principles embodied in the heart of the Eighth Route Army are the principles that will guide and save China, that will give the greatest of impulses to the liberation of all subjected Asiatic nations and bring to life a new human society.' While at the front Agnes finished a new book 'China Fights Back' before leaving for Hanzhou in 1938.

After meeting Dr K S Lim, director and founder of the Chinese Red Cross Medical Corps in Hanzhou. Agnes immediately joined the corps as a publicity worker. Because most of China's 10,000 doctors remained in private practice in the littoral cities or in the Japanese occupied regions, her first duty was to help recruit foreign medical volunteers. Dr Norman Bethune was among those she enlisted.

"I don't know what happened to her after that," Bethune said.

"I do," I said. "Thanks to the internet."

In mid-1938 Agnes became a special wartime correspondent for the Manchester Guardian. During her travels with the New Fourth Army (formed from Red guerrillas left behind when the, main body of the Red Army left for the Long March in 1934 and who were re-assembled for operation in the Japanese rear), she lectured and inspected hospitals and reported on the extent of American aid to the Japanese war machine. The activities of the American war merchants were summed up by the General Li Chungren (acting President in the last days of KMT rule after Chiang fled to Taiwan 1949-50): 'The Japanese murderers were without a sword. America gave them the sword.'

In ill health and unable to stay with the guerrillas Agnes decided to leave China in 1941 and go back to the US. There she completed her new book 'Battle Hymn of China' in 1943. She spent many years lecturing and writing about China's plight and desperate need for medical aid and publicized to the American people the corruption of the KMT and western imperialism in China.

It was part of an effort to silence such objective reporting on China that General MacArthur's headquarters in Tokyo released a fifty-four page spy report on a Soviet spy ring in Japan, naming Agnes as 'a Soviet spy ... still at large.' The source of this charge was the twenty year old files of the Imperial Japanese secret police! Agnes insisted that MacArthur was making an issue of the spy ring at that particular time because of the defeat of Chiang Kai-shek, and that his aim was to 'condition the American people into allowing him' more troops and money to build Japan into a mighty military base. (New York Times, February 1949)

Eight days later Washington was forced to retract the 'faux pas' but the damage was more than done to Agnes. Due to the smear Agnes could no longer lecture nor sell articles nor even find a place to live. She tried to sue MacArthur for libel but he remained protected by diplomatic 'immunity'. Her health broken, Agnes finally obtained a passport to England where she died on 8 May, 1950, without completing her last book 'The Great Road, the Life and Times of Zhu De'. Although she longed to return to China, it was a year after her death before she was accorded her last wish: 'As my heart and spirit have found no rest in any other land on earth except China, I wish my ashes to lie with the Chinese Revolutionary dead.' She was buried in Beijing.

Chapter Two. Past Life #2: Marco Polo Meets Kubla Khan

"In Xanadu did Kubla Khan
A stately pleasure-dome decree"
- Samuel Taylor Coleridge

Nevermore shall I return
Escape these caves of ice
For I have dined on honey dew
And drunk the milk of Paradise
- Rush

The first time I did any Past Life work, or traveled in time, was the first time that China caught my interest.

As a kid, I was told I had to eat everything on my plate because people were starving in China, which made no sense to me, but when I was in Grade Five, I think, we learned about Marco Polo and his adventures in China.

Before that, when I went to Santa's Village, the little Christmas theme park in the town beside ours, I was shown the longest rope in the world, which had one end tied to a big white pine tree and the other end went underground, all the way to China, I was told. It was right beside a pond filled with invisible goldfish.

Ever since then, China, goldfish, the other side of the world, Christmas, and Santa Claus have been connected, in my mind, and when I was in Grade 5, Marco Polo got added to that last, along with Kublai Khan.

We learned a lot about Kublai Khan and his empire. He led the Mongols and they took over China. They were centred in the north-west, or Dongbei, and controlled a lot of the land that is now called China.

Kublai Khan, born Kublai and also known by the temple name Shizu, was the fifth Khagan (Great Khan) of the Ikh Mongol Uls, reigning from 1260 to 1294, and the founder of the Yuan Dynasty. The Mongolian general and statesman Kublai Khan was the grandson of Genghis Khan. He conquered China and became the first emperor of its Yuan, or Mongol, dynasty.

Marco Polo was an explorer from Italy who traveled around the Mongol empire and reported back to Kublai Khan, telling him all about the different cities he visited. He would also tell the Kublai Khan how much the people in those places liked their emperor. I really liked reading about Kublai Khan, the Mongols, Marco Polo, and China in that era, and about "Genghis Khan," who started the Mongol invasions that resulted in the conquest of most of Eurasia, or most of the known world, at that time. He was vilified throughout most of history for the brutality of his campaigns, but was also credited with bringing the Silk Road under one cohesive political environment. Increased communication and trade from Northeast Asia to Southwest Asia and Christian Europe expanded the horizons of all three areas.

Fast forward a decade to the time I was in high school and read the famous poem called Kublai Khan, by Samuel Taylor Coleridge. We were fascinated by the fact that the poem was composed one night after Coleridge experienced an opium-influenced dream after reading a work describing Xanadu, the summer palace of the Mongol ruler and Emperor of China, Kublai Khan.

Fast forward another decade to the time I was in university and discovered a book I liked a lot by an Italian author who reminded me of me, quite a bit, and who wrote a book called Invisible Cities that was all about Marco Polo, his travels, and his reports to Kublai Khan.

Once again, I felt a strange connection to China. It felt as though I was there, in China, at the time of Marco Polo and Kublai Khan.

I remembered all that when I moved to China and did some Past Life work. First I discovered I had a past life in China in the time of Dr. Norman Bethune, and then I went back further in time. I was living in Dongbei, in Dalian, China, in an area that had been Manchuria and, before that, part of the Mongol Empire. I met people from Inner Mongolia and people who traveled to Outer Mongolia.

As kids in school, we learned that the Gobi Desert was a big part of Mongolia. My oldest brother came back from his first year at university with a sweatshirt that had Gobi Desert Canoe Club printed on it.

I spent a long time trying to figure out what that meant, when I was five or six years old.

After living in China for several months, I asked some Chinese people what they thought of Marco Polo.

Shenma? they said. What? Who's that?

I asked them about Kublai Khan.

They said they did not think much about him because he was not a great emperor. He wasn't Chinese. He was very wealthy but the people in this part of the world did not have very good lives or get wealthy while he was the emperor, they told me, so they did not think much of him.

They had another name for Marco Polo, of course, which was the name the Chinese people gave him at the time.

Undeterred, I wanted to discover whatever I could about my connection to the time of Marco Polo and Kublai Khan, so I did some past life work aimed at that era.
First, I went to the museum in Jinshitan, to see if they had Marco Polo or Kublai Khan in wax.

They had Genghis Khan.

Seeing Genghis Khan in a museum made me think of an American movie called Night At The Museum, with Ben Stiller, and about Attila The Hun, who was a character in that movie.

It made me wonder: Who was the bigger figure? Who would win a fight between Genghis Khan and Attila The Hun?

Genghis Khan had a bigger army. But what would happen in a fight between the two of them. Picture: Genghis Khan versus Attila The Hun, mano-a-mano, one-on-one.

Next, I went for a walk on the beach in Jinshitan and imagined that the beach went on forever in both directions. It is a beautiful beach on the Yellow Sea with the Black Mountains as a backdrop. I picked a day in May when the weather was perfect for walking on the beach and the water temperature was just the way I like it for wading in the sea. I walked and walked and imagined walking even further so that I traveled in time as well as in space.

I went back to the day before, the week before, the month before, and the year before. I went back to the decade before and the century before, in that place, now called Jinshitan, and kept going back in time until I was walking with Marco Polo to meet Kublai Khan for a picnic on the beach with the golden sand.

Marco Polo was writing a report about the place. It was a beautiful bay in an area that was just wild. There were fishing villages up and down the coast but no big towns, never mind the kind of city he liked to visit. Marco Polo liked to report on the industries and specialities of the cities he wrote about for Kublai Khan, so he could say, this place is famous for this spice, and this place is famous for that mineral, and so on.

This place was famous for fish and for seaweed. There were many types of thick, green, weeds growing in the sea that could be harvested and used as food for people and for animals. It grew close to shore and could be harvested easily, in great quantities, and tasted good with a lot of fish dishes, if you cooked it for a while and added some spices. There were so many species of fish in the Yellow Sea by the bay with the golden pebbles, it was like finding gold, he told me.

I looked down at the ground as we walked, so I could see my feet, and my shoes, to get some idea of who I was, and why I might be walking along the beach with Marco Polo, on the way to meet Kublai Khan.

We were both barefoot, walking along the shore, but we held fancy-looking sandals in our hands. We spoke Italian and our sandals looked different than the sandals worn by the people collecting seaweed and bringing in boatloads of fish.

Were our sandals made in Italy?

Marco Polo spoke Chinese, as well as Italian, and so did I, I realized.

Marco Polo accompanied his father on a trip to China and was probably the best-known foreign visitor ever to set foot in China, until Dr. Bethune. He spent 17 years in China, working for Kublai Khan. The popularity of his journal, Description of the World, generated unprecedented enthusiasm in Europe for going east.

Marco Polo was complaining about something. He told me Kublai Khan was sick, or had a sore back, or sore feet, or sore legs, or something.

The guy who conquered China has a bad back? I said.

Kublai Khan completed the conquest of China, but most of China had been conquered by previous Mongol Great Khans, not Kublai, Marco Polo informed me.

He's basically a nomad, he added. He conquered the Song dynasty and established a great capital city, called Beijing, which is where I met him.

Kublai Khan was the fourth son of Tulë, one of the four sons of Genghis by his favourite wife, Bourtai. Strong, brave, and intelligent, Kublai was Genghis's favorite grandson; when he was only a lad, he had accompanied his father, Tulë, in campaigns. He invited men of culture to his quarters in Karakorum in the Gobi Desert to find out about political affairs in China, including the famous Buddho-Taoist Liu Ping-chung, who advised him on the Confucian principles of government and the application of Chinese methods for administrative and economic reforms.

Under Kublai, religious establishments of the Buddhist, Taoist, Nestorian, and Islamic orders were all exempted from taxation, and their clergy acquired local land rights and economic privileges. The Chinese indigenous religion, Neo-Taoism, was popular under Kublai, although it faced continuous challenge from the Buddhists.

He was the fifth Khagan (Great Khan) of the Ikh Mongol Uls (Mongol Empire), reigning from 1260 to 1294, and the founder of the Yuan Dynasty, a division of the Mongol Empire, and the Emperor of China.

As for the back pain .... It came and went, he said, so he thought he might be crazy.

Ah, I heard myself say, in Chinese. A sore back .... A lot of people complain about that .... But there are quite a few things you can do to make things better .... It's all about the centre part of the back but it can make everything below it hurt quite a bit ....
He has to keep it warm, eat hot food, and drink hot drinks.

As soon as I saw Kublai Khan, I told Marco Polo, You have to tell him to lose weight. -- His back and legs and so on won't bother him so much if he loses some weight. -- Or a lot of weight.

I'm not going to tell him that, Marco Polo said, and you shouldn't tell him that, either.

Well, we've got to get the information to him somehow, I said, if we want to help him.

Marco Polo looked at me blankly as an undressed pizza or jian bing.

Do you want to help him? I asked.

I want him to help me, Marco Polo said. So I want to give him the impression that I'm helping him.

Ah, I said. I see. Well .... Come with me.

We got some of the guys who were harvesting seaweed to give me some and we got some fishermen to build a fire so I could heat it up. I found something to wrap it in -- a tunic with long sleeves -- so it could be wrapped around him.

Apparently I was some sort of healer who traveled around China with Marco Polo and helped Kublai Khan with his sore back.

"Marco?" I said.

"Polo," he answered.

That made me laugh.

"What's so funny?" he asked me.

I told him that, in the future, millions of people would say his name when they were looking for each other in dark or crowded places. One says "Marco" and the other answers "Polo" so they can get together.

"The future?" Marco Polo said.

"Yes," I said. "Later, there will be an app. for your cellphone that helps you find your phone, when you misplace it. You say "Marco" and the phone answers "Polo!"

"What are you talking about?" Marco Polo said. "Have you lost your mind? Or have you really been to the future?"

"Yes," I said. "You traveled from Italy to China, and all around China, but I travel in time."

"Oh really," he said, sounding skeptical. "Tell me," he said, "What are the cities like in the future."

I told him China had cities with over ten million people. There were huge cities around the world, including New York, Tokyo, and Beijing.

He wanted details so I gave him a list of the top twenty cities in the world, with their populations, in round numbers:

1. Tokyo, Japan (37,126,000)

2. Jakarta, Indonesia (26,063,000)

3. Seoul, South Korea (22,547,000)

4. Delhi, India (22,242,000)

5. Shanghai, China (20,860,000)

6. Manila, Philippines (20,767,000)

7. Karachi, Pakistan (20,711,000)

8. New York, USA (20,464,000)

9. Sao Paulo, Brazil (20,186,000)

10. Mexico City, Mexico (19,463,000)

11. Cairo, Egypt (17,816,000)

12. Beijing, China (17,311,000)

13. Osaka, Japan (17,011,000)

14. Mumbai (Bombay), India (16,910,000)

15. Guangzhou, China (16,827,000)

16. Moscow, Russia (15,512,000)

17. Los Angeles, USA (14,900,000)

18. Calcutta, India (14,374,000)

19. Dhaka, Bangladesh (14,000,000)

20. Buenos Aires, Argentina (13,639,000)

I told him that the place where we were standing, on the beach with golden sand and stones, would be called JinShiTan and it would be part of a city called Dalian, and Dalian would have a population of six million people, just like the biggest city in Canada, which was called Toronto.

That made him laugh hard.

Six million people! he said. There aren't six million people in the whole world!

There's about half a billion, now, I told him. There will be six billion by the year 2000 and ten billion by the year 2050 ....

China will be the biggest country in the world, with one and a half billion people, I told him.

When will that happen? he asked me.

The twenty first century, I said.

When do the cities of the world stop fighting and join together to create these countries you talk about? he asked me.

"Well," I said, "Genghis Khan conquered most of Asia and created an empire that was like one big country, joined together by The Silk Road, and his grandson, here, Kublai Khan has kept it going. The city states you know, from your travels in Italy and the rest of Europe, join together to form different countries, but then those countries go to war."

"Don't tell me any more," he said. "It sounds horrible!"

"Well," I said, "in the twentieth century, there are two world wars, followed by a cold war, and a lot of other wars, but after World War One and World War Two, the people of the planet managed to avoid World War Three. But then the weather went wild ...."

"Stop!" he said. "I don't want to travel in time! I just want to go back home to Venice!"

"It could happen," I assured him.

Chapter 3. Past Life #3: Buddhadhabra And Bodhidharma

Emperor Wu: "How much karmic merit have I earned for ordaining Buddhist monks, building monasteries, having sutras copied, and commissioning Buddha images?" Bodhidharma: "None. Good deeds done with worldly intent bring good karma, but no merit." Emperor Wu: "So what is the highest meaning of noble truth?" Bodhidharma: "There is no noble truth, there is only emptiness." Emperor Wu: "Then, who is standing before me?"
Bodhidharma: "I know not, Your Majesty."

The first time I showed up at the Zen Forest, in the Far East of Ontario, in Canada, the monk and Zen master Thich Thong Tri Thay did a double-take and said, "Oh! I thought you were Bodhidarma!"
I took it as a compliment, as I knew who he was: the mysterious spiritual man from India who took Zen to China. Later, I learned that, in Asia, he was regarded differently than in the West. He was a big, hairy, blue-eyed, bearded guy who looked like a barbarian and was considered quite ugly. To this day, his picture appears in martial arts training halls around the world. He is know for kungfu and the martial arts that originated with the exercises he taught the monks at Shaolin Temple in China.
Ever since that moment when the monk and Zen master in Canada mistook me for the blue-eyed, bearded, Bodhidarma, I've felt a special connection to the big lug who lived in a cave and meditated like a madman.
The story of the Shaolin monks is world-famous and in recent years their fame has grown thanks to many martial arts, kungfu, and Shaolin movies. I had already written a book about Shaolin hockey, with a team of Canadian kids who go from worst to first by studying, practicing, and using kungfu on the ice, when playing Canada's number one game.

Shaolin Kung Fu has been world renown for its physical artistry and prowess and these movies capture the style's impressive look. Fans of martial arts movies respect the complex and mysterious world of Shaolin Kung Fu and the people who practice it. Every frame explodes with the electricity generated from these Shaolin Kung Fu movies through every battle and foe that comes in their path. Here are the five best Shaolin Kung Fu movies:

In "War of the Shaolin Temple" (1980), the advancing Manchu army seeks to destroy the temple and its 3,000 inhabitants without mercy. The monks decide to confront the foreign army in a series of one-on-one duels to the death.

In "The Shaolin Temple" (1982), a martial arts movie of intrigue about the assassination of the Tang emperor by a traitorous general, Jet Li starred as one of his slave workers flees to a Shaolin Temple and learns Kung Fu in order to avenge the death of his master.

In "The 36th Chamber of Shaolin" (1978), a young man survives an attack by the Manchus and devotes his life to learning the martial arts with deadly precision. He takes his newfound knowledge and goes out on a quest for revenge against the Manchus.

In "Five Masters of Death" (1974), patriots escape the horrific attack on the Shaolin Temple by the Qing army. They return to the charred ruins of the temple to hone their skills and seek revenge against the Qing's best warriors.

In "Shaolin Soccer" (2001), a former soccer star hooks up with a Shaolin Kung Fu student who travels the land to teach martial arts. They combine their skills to create a unique form of soccer to compete against the best in the field.

The list of movies about Shaolin continues to grow.

Shaolin, released in the Hong Kong as The New Shaolin Temple, was a 2011 Chinese-Hong Kong martial arts film starring Jackie Chan.

Shaolin Monastery or Shaolin Temple is a Chán or Zen Buddhist temple on Mount Song, near Dengfeng, Zhengzhou, Henan province, China, tounded in the fifth century. The monastery has long been famous for its association with Chinese martial arts and particularly with Shaolin Kung Fu. It is the best known Mahayana Buddhist monastery to the Western world.

Shaolin Monastery and its famed Pagoda Forest were inscribed as a UNESCO World Heritage Site in 2010 as part of the "Historic Monuments of Dengfeng."

The shào in "Shaolin" refers to Shaoshi Mountain, one of the seven mountains forming the Songshan mountain range; it is on this mountain the Temple is situated. The word lín means "forest". The word sì means "monastery or temple".

Shaolin was incorrectly translated as "young or new forest" or sometimes "little forest" and that translation is commonly accepted today.

After climbing the 1500 steps up Dàhēi Shān, on the path I called The Stairway To Heaven, I took a motorcycle taxi over to the temple called Dragon Spits On Lotus, so I could meditate in front of the dragon and do some more past life work. I wanted to go back in time to the year 555 AD, half a century after the Indian monk Ba Tuo, or Buddhabhadra, founded the Shaolin Temple on the land given to him at the foot of Shaoshi Mountain.

I was one of the monks at Shaolin. I looked down at the dusty stone steps I was standing on and saw my feet in sandals, cracked and dry, and just when I was wondering who I was I heard somebody cry, "Hey, Buddhadabra!"

I had a name!

"Make me some dhebra!" the same guy called.

It turned out he was from Gujarat, in India, and you know what they say: Gujjus and snacks can never be parted!

Gujaratis do make the best snacks, I discovered. Dhebra is an easy and amazing yogurt and ginger dish that has been popular for a long time in Gujarat.

My buddy gave me the recipe for dhebra.

Come on, he said. We will make it together. It will only take a few minutes.

It took more than a few minutes.

It took several minutes.

But it was worth it.

And it takes longer if you have to make the dough at the same time.

The resting time for the dough is fifteen to thirty minutes.

His recipe makes several servings.

Here's the list of ingredients:

Whole Wheat Flour (Chapati Flour) – 1 cup

Millet Flour (Bajra) – 1/3 cup

Yogurt – 1/2 cup

Citric Acid – 1/4 tsp (if the yogurt is not sour)

Jaggery (Gud) or Brown Sugar – 1 tbsp

Minced Ginger – 2 tsp

Minced Garlic – 2 tsp

Sesame Seeds – 1 tbsp

Cumin Powder -1/2 tsp

Turmeric Powder – 1/4 tsp

Red Chili Powder – 1/4 tsp or to taste

Green Chillies – to taste (minced)

Salt – 1 tsp or to taste

Kasoori Methi (Dried Fenugreek Leaves) – 2 tbsp

Cilantro (Coriander Leaves) – 1/4 cup

Oil – 2 tbsp

Oil – for pan frying

Here's how you do it:

1. Combine Yogurt, Citric Acid, and Jaggery or Brown Sugar in a big bowl.

2. Mix well and break down all the lumps.

3. Add Ginger, Garlic, Sesame Seeds, Cumin Powder, Turmeric Powder, Red Chili Powder, Green Chillies, Salt, Kasoori Methi (Dried Fenugreek Leaves) and Cilantro (Coriander Leaves).

4. Mix again and set aside.

5. To make the dough, combine the the flours, add the Oil (2 tbsp) and work the Oil into the flour till well incorporated.

6. Add in the Yogurt/Spice mixture and make a dough without using any additional Water.

7. Once the fours come together in a dough, knead for a few minutes.

8. Drizzle a few drops of Oil on the dough, cover and allow the dough to rest for 15 – 30 minutes.

9. Heat a Tawa on medium heat till nice and hot.

10. Divide the dough and make golf size balls.

11. Take one and form a smooth ball and then flatten with your palms.

12. Dust in some Whole Wheat Flour and start rolling it with a rolling pin on a flat surface.

13. Keep dusting while rolling as needed.

14. Roll it out similar to Chapati in thickness.

15. Once done rolling, dust off excess Flour and place it on the hot tawa.

16. Move the Dhebra a little so it does not stick and the allow it to cook on the underside till you see a few bubbles appear.

17. Once the bubbles are visible, flip the Dhebra and allow it to cool on the other side.

18. Drizzle a little bit of Oil, spread it and flip it.

19. Press down gently but firmly with a flat spatula – pressing and turning as you go.

20. Apply Oil on this side as well and flip and press down again.

21. Take off the tawa and transfer into an insulated container till ready to eat.

Tips: Make a big batch and store in the refrigerator and use as needed. They have a great shelf-life. Take it on long or short road trips or hikes in the mountains. It travels well.

While we were making dhebra, I got my Buddhist buddy to tell me all about Shaolin. He told me that was the name of the place we were in.

Around the time that Ba Tuo was founding the Shaolin Temple there was an Indian prince named Bodhidharma, he said, and Bodhidharma was the favourite son of the king of a region that is now part of southern India. Bodhidharma was very smart. He had two older brothers who feared that their father, the king, would pass them over and bequeath the kingship to Bodhidharma. The jealous brothers often made fun of Bodhidharma while talking with their father, hoping to turn him against the younger brother.

The older brothers also attempted to assassinate Bodhidharma but Bodhidharma had very good karma, so the attempts were not successful.

Despite being the favorite son of the king, Bodhidharma realized he wasn't interested in a life of politics. He chose instead to study with the famous Buddhist master Prajnatara and become a Buddhist monk.

Bodhidharma trained with his master for many years. One day he asked his master, "Master, when you pass away, where should I go? What should I do?"

His master replied that he should go to Zhen Dan, which was the name for China.

Years later, Bodhidharma's master passed away and Bodhidharma prepared to leave for China.

During the many years Bodhidharma studied as a monk, one of his brothers became king of India. That older brother's son became king after him. The king of India was very fond of his uncle and wanted to make amends for the actions which his big brothers had taken against him.

He asked Bodhidharma to stay near the capital, where he could protect and care for him, but Bodhidharma knew that he must go to China as his master had said.

Seeing that Bodhidharma would not remain, the king of India ordered that carrier pigeons be sent to China with messages asking the people of China to take care of Bodhidharma.

These messages made Bodhidharma famous among many Chinese who wondered what was so special about this particular Buddhist monk that the king of India would make such a request.

Bodhidharma traveled from India to China by way of some of the other countries in southeast Asia. In China, he was known as Da Mo.

He arrived in China practicing Da Sheng (Mahayana) Buddhism. When he arrived, he was greeted by a large crowd of people who had heard of the famous Buddhist master and wished to hear him speak.

However, instead of speaking, Da Mo sat down and meditated.

He meditated for many hours.

Upon completing his meditation, Da Mo rose and walked away, saying nothing.

His actions had a profound effect upon his audience. Some people laughed, some cried, some were angry and some nodded their heads in understanding. Regardless of the emotion, everyone in the crowd had a reaction.

This was a very famous story, but I liked hearing it first hand, from somebody who said he was actually in the audience when Do Mo spoke. Or refused to speak.

That incident made Da Mo even more famous.

He was so famous that Emperor Wu heard of him.

Emperor Wu, who ruled over the southern kingdom of China, invited Da Mo to come to his palace. When Da Mo arrived, Emperor Wu talked with Da Mo about Buddhism.

The emperor had erected many statues and temples devoted to Buddhism. He had given a lot of money to Buddhist temples. While talking of his accomplishments, Emperor Wu asked Da Mo if his actions were good.

Da Mo replied that they were not.

That response surprised Emperor Wu, but they continued talking and eventually Emperor Wu asked Da Mo if there was Buddha in this world.

Da Mo replied that there was not.

Da Mo's replies were a reflection of Emperor Wu. By asking if his actions were good, Emperor Wu was searching for compliments and affirmation from Da Mo.

However, Da Mo pointed out that Emperor Wu's actions were not good as it was the duty of the emperor to care for his people.

Rather than seeking compliments, Emperor Wu should have been content to help his people.

Similarly, if one asks if there is Buddha in the world, then one has already answered the question: Buddha is a matter of faith, you either believe in your heart or you do not.

In questioning the existence of Buddha, Emperor Wu had demonstrated a lack of faith.

Da Mo's answers enraged Emperor Wu and he ordered Da Mo to leave his palace and never return.

Da Mo simply smiled, turned and left.

Da Mo continued his journey, heading north, when he reached the city of Nanjing.

In Nanjing, there was a famous place called the Flower Rain Pavillion where many people gathered to speak and relax. There was a large crowd of people gathered in the Flower Rain Pavillion around a Buddhist monk, who was lecturing.

This Buddhist monk, named Shen Guang, had been a famous general. He had killed many people in battle but one day realized that the people he had been killing had family and friends and that one day someone might come and kill him. This changed him and he decided to train as a Buddhist monk.

Eventually, Shen Guang became a great speaker on Buddhism.

As Da Mo neared the crowd, he listened to Shen Guang's speech.

Sometimes Shen Guang would speak and Da Mo would nod his head, as if in agreement. Sometimes Shen Guang would speak and Da Mo would shake his head, as if in disagreement. As this continued, Shen Guang became very angry at the strange foreign monk who dared to disagree with him in front of this crowd.

In anger, Shen Guang took the Buddhist beads from around his neck and flicked them at Da Mo.

The beads struck Da Mo in his face, knocking out two of his front teeth.

Da Mo immediately began bleeding.

Shen Guang expected a confrontation; instead, Da Mo smiled, turned and walked away.

This reaction astounded Shen Guang, who began following after Da Mo.

He left Nanjing and continued north until he reached the Yangzi river.

Seated by the river there was an old woman with a large bundle of reeds next to her. Da Mo walked up to the old woman and asked her if he might have a reed. She replied that he might.

Da Mo took a single reed, placed it upon the surface of the Yangzi river and stepped onto the reed. He was carried across the Yangzi river by the force of his chi.

Seeing this, Shen Guang ran up to where the old woman sat and grabbed a handful of reeds without asking.

He threw the reeds onto the Yangzi river and stepped onto them. The reeds sank beneath him and Shen Guang began drowning.

The old woman saw his plight and took pity on Shen Guang, pulling him from the river. As Shen Guang lay on the ground coughing up river water, the old woman admonished him. She said that by not asking for her reeds before taking them, he had shown her disrespect and that by disrespecting her, Shen Guang had disrespected himself.

The old woman also told Shen Guang that he had been searching for a master and that Da Mo, the man he was following, was that master.

As she said this, the reeds which had sunk beneath Shen Guang rose again to the surface of the river and Shen Guang found himself on the reeds being carried across the Yangzi river. He reached the other side and continued following after Da Mo.

There are many people who believe that the old woman by the river was a Boddhisatva who was helping Shen Guang to end the cycle of his samsara.

At this point, Da Mo was nearing the location of the Shaolin Temple.

The Shaolin monks had heard of his approach and were gathered to meet him.

When Da Mo arrived, the Shaolin monks greeted him and invited him to come stay at the temple. Da Mo did not reply but he went to a cave on a mountain behind the Shaolin Temple, sat down, and began meditating.

In front of the Shaolin Temple, there are five mountains: Bell Mountain, Drum Mountain, Sword Mountain, Stamp Mountain and Flag Mountain. These mountains are named after the objects which their shape resembles.

Behind the Shaolin Temple there are five "Breast Mountains" which are shaped like breasts.

The cave in which Da Mo chose to meditate was on one of the Breast Mountains.

Da Mo sat facing a wall in the cave and meditated for nine years.

During these nine years, Shen Guang stayed outside Da Mo's cave and acted as a bodyguard for Da Mo, ensuring that no harm came to Da Mo.

Periodically Shen Guang would ask Da Mo to teach him, but Da Mo never responded to Shen Guang's requests.

During these nine years the Shaolin monks would also periodically invite Da Mo to come down to the Temple, where he would be much more comfortable, but Da Mo never responded.

After some time, they say Da Mo's concentration became so intense that his image was engraved into the stone of the wall before him.

Towards the end of the nine years, the Shaolin monks decided that they must do something more for Da Mo and so they made a special room for him.

They called this room the Da Mo Ting.

When this room was completed at the end of the nine years, the Shaolin monks invited Da Mo to come stay in the room.

Da Mo did not respond but he stood up, walked down to the room, sat down, and immediately began meditating.

Shen Guang followed Da Mo to the Shaolin temple and stood guard outside Da Mo's room. Da Mo meditated in his room for another four years.

Shen Guang would occasionally ask Da Mo to teach him, but Da Mo never responded.

At the end of the four-year period Shen Guang had been following Da Mo for thirteen years, but Da Mo had never said anything to Shen Guang. It was winter, Shen Guang was standing in the snow outside the window to Da Mo's room, cold and angry.

He picked up a large block of snow and ice and hurled it into Da Mo's room.

The snow and ice made a loud noise as it broke inside Da Mo's room.

This noise awoke Da Mo from his meditation.

He looked at Shen Guang.

In anger and frustration Shen Guang demanded to know when Da Mo would teach him.

Da Mo said he would teach Shen Guang when red snow fell from the sky.

Hearing this, something inside Shen Guang changed. He took a sword he carried and cut off his left arm.

He held the severed arm above his head and whirled it around. The blood from the arm froze in the cold air and fell like red snow. Seeing this, Da Mo agreed to teach Shen Guang.

I have heard and read this story dozens of times.

It never gets any better.

Da Mo took a monk's spade and went with Shen Guang to the Drum Mountain in front of Shaolin Temple. Drum Mountain is very flat on top. Da Mo's unspoken message to Shen Guang was that Shen Guang should flatten his heart, just like the surface of the Drum Mountain.

On this Drum Mountain Da Mo dug a well. The water of this well was bitter. Da Mo then left Shen Guang on the Drum Mountain. For an entire year, Shen Guang used the bitter water of the well to take care of all of his needs. He used it to cook, to clean, to bathe, to do everything.

At the end of the first year, Shen Guang went down to Da Mo and again asked Da Mo to teach him.

Da Mo returned with Shen Guang to the Drum Mountain and dug a second well.

The water of this well was spicy.

For an entire year, Shen Guang used the spicy water for all of his needs. At the end of the second year, Shen Guang went back down to Da Mo and asked again to be taught.

Da Mo dug a third well on the Drum Mountain.

The water of this third well was sour.

For the third year, Shen Guang used the sour water for all of his needs.

At the end of the third year, Shen Guang returned to Da Mo and agains asked to be taught.

Da Mo returned to the Drum Mountain and dug a fourth and final well. The water of this well was sweet.

At this point, Shen Guang realized that the four wells represented his life. Like the wells, his life would sometimes be bitter, sometimes sour, sometimes spicy and sometimes sweet.

Each of these phases in his life was equally beautiful and necessary, just as each of the four seasons of the year is beautiful and necessary in its own way. Without really saying many words to Shen Guang, Da Mo had taught Shen Guang the most important of lessons in a mind-to-mind, heart-to-heart fashion. This mind-to- mind, heart-to-heart communication is called "action language" and is the foundation of the Chan Buddhism which Da Mo began at the Shaolin Temple.

After his realization, Shen Guang was given the name Hui Ke and he became abbot of the Shaolin temple after Da Mo.

To pay respect for the sacrifice which Hui Ke made, disciples and monks of the Shaolin Temple greet each other using only their right hand.

This gory story has always horrified me.

Was it a true story? Or just a legend. Or a parable.

I'd always wanted to go back in time to hear Buddha and Jesus speak, and to hear Bodhidharma speak, or not speak.

When I returned to the here and now, at the Taoist temple I called Dragon Spits On Lotus, I reflected on my time at Shaolin and my time in the Zen Forest.

I thought it was ironic that the monk and Zen master at the Zen Forest did a double-take when he saw me, thinking I might be Bodhidharma.

I thought about all the great teachers I had worked with and thought about which teacher I would have cut off my left arm in order to impress them enough so they would take me as a student.

-- Still thinking ....

Chapter 4. Past Life #4: Peking Man Eating Peking Duck

".., for I am a sensitive man ...." -- Canadian poet, Al Purdy

When I lived and worked in Northern Alberta, in the oil patch, or the tar sands, last year, I thought about the dinosaurs quite a bit. The dinosaurs died to give us oil: that's the slogan of the tar patch. My apartment was what we called a "man cave": a one bedroom, bachelor, decorated with memorabilia from the Edmonton Eskimos of the Canadian Football League and the Edmonton Oilers of the National Hockey League, as well as the Saskatchewan Roughriders, not to mention the Saskatoon Sirens of the LFL (that's the Lingerie Football League!). From my balcony, I had a great view of the sunrise and sunset on the flat Canadian prairie. I loved driving down to Edmonton for the weekend in the winter when you followed the setting sun for hours and the whole world looked as though it had turned to gold.

The drive up to Fort MacMurray, on the Highway of Death, and then up to Fort Chip, on the ice highway, was something else. I liked traveling along Highway 55, from Cold Lake to Lac La Biche, on the 55th parallel, with only wilderness to the north, until you got to .... Russia.

When I wasn't working, I re-read a lot of Canadian literature, starting with Margaret Atwood. She has been criticized, at times, for having male characters with monosyllabic names that sound like grunts and personalities as complex as the early hunters and gatherers of the caveman days. Alberta men have been criticized, at times, for being like Atwood characters.

When I lived in Muskoka, only halfway between the equator and the North Pole, on the 45th parallel of latitude, I was the Arts Department Head at the high school. That was the region I came from. I still have great memories of my time at Bracebridge and Muskoka Lakes Secondary School. My soccer team went to the All-Ontario championship and my hockey team won the provincial championship. I dreamt about playing for Canada's national team, in the days before NHL players were allowed to play in the Olympics, even though the Ruskies used their best players, claiming they were amateurs because they were employed by the army, although the whole world knew their job was to play hockey.

The team I played for was called the Indians and we used the logo, colours, chest crest, and shoulder flashes of the Chicago Blackhawks: an aboriginal in war paint was plastered over my heart and crossed stone clubs decorated my shoulders.

In Muskoka, in summer, as kids, we were free to run all over town, from Lake Muskoka to Gull Lake, which included Look Out Park, with its caves, but we were not allowed to play by the Rock Crusher, which was what the locals called a pair of abandoned concrete towers, so we ran over there, across Highway 69, to play in the caves of the granite ridge at the edge of town all the time.

I loved going over to the Blue Mountains of Collingwood, beside the longest freshwater beach in the world, to explore the caves around the area called Ekarenniondo, which we were told means "where the earth touches heaven". My favourite was the ice cave, which was so cold, even in the middle of summer, when it was 90 degrees outside, there was still ice inside the old granite walls.

The Muskoka Mountains, we were told, were an ancient range, once greater than the Rockies, but eroded, over time, by the ice ages.

In short, I have always identified with cave men.

In school, I loved learning about the dinosaurs, as most boys do, but instead of collecting Matchbox cars, minis, and Tonka toys that were tiny work vehicles with everything needed at a small-scale construction site, I collected dinosaurs.

I liked to mix my dinos with Matchbox cars, to have T-Rex stomping on an Austin Mini, or a brontasauras dueling with a cement mixer.

My best friend, my buddy from across the street, and I loved to pretend we were dinosaurs, acting like the infamous Muskoka-saurus, which I made up.

So, it was not surprising, to me, that when I did past life work while living in China, half a century later, I went way back in time to meet Peking Man.

In China, there are areas where people still live in caves, on the other side of Beijing from where I lived, in Dalian. I wanted to go back to the time people lived only in caves. I wanted to eat Peking Duck with Peking Man.

As an anthropology student at the University of Victoria, we studied the old bones that gave us the theory that has been popularized as "out of Africa", but I never fully believed that all of mankind had the same ancestry, like Adam, or Noah, or Lucy, or some black Charlie Brown character who looked more like an ape or an orangutang. In my bones, I felt I should believe in the idea that mankind evolved separately in Africa, Asia, and Muskoka, or North America, as well as Europe and different places in England, Scotland, and Ireland, as well as Wales.

It wasn't a scientific theory, just a feeling, based somewhat on my personal experience, meeting people from those areas.

I'm not saying I grew up with a bunch of Neanderthals, playing hockey in Gravenhurst, Muskoka, Ontario, and Canada, but my sister made that claim, from time to time.

We won the Little NHL Tournament, down south in Wingham, playing against teams from the U.S.A., including the Northern Illinois All-Star League, a team with the letters N.I.H.L. on their hockey sweaters. We annihilated the NIHLs in the Little NHL like nihilists.

I joined a hockey team called The Ice Dragons, in China, when I moved to Dalian, and went up north to play Canada's number one game in Harbin, which used to be part of the Gulag Archipelego in the dark days of the U.S.S.R.

Actually, Harbin was such a horrible place in those days they would let you out of the Gulag if the agreed to move there.

Now it's a great big city with a fabulous ice festival that rivals the more famous one in Quebec City. The Indians went to the peewee hockey tournament at the Quebec Winter Carnival when I was a kid and the Ice Dragons went to the men's tournament at the Harbin Winter Carnival when I was in my second or third childhood.

The Ice Dragons won a big tournament for ex-pat teams in Beijing and brought back the Bethune Cup.

Yes, China's version of the Stanley Cup is named after my hero, Dr. Norman Bethune, whose birthplace -- Gravenhurst -- is my old hometown.

Whenever I go to Beijing, which is just a one hour flight from Dalian, or an overnight train ride, I go for Peking Duck, of course, and think about Peking Man.

Personally, I prefer Peking Duck in Dalian, but there is something about getting Peking Duck in Beijing, the big city we used to call Peking, that makes it seem more special.

Few people call it Beijing Duck.

Few people refer to Peking Man as Beijing Man.

Beijing has several hockey teams with odd names, but not one of them picked the name "Peking Ducks".

Oddly enough, there are no hockey teams anywhere named after cavemen.

The Norwegian Neanderthals would strike fear into the hearts of all competitors.

Not.

The Canadian Cavemen would scare the crap out of everybody.

The Beijing Hockey League could have the Peking Ducks versus the Peking Men in the play-offs for the Bethune Cup.

Needless to say, when I did past life work on Dàhēi Shān, in the ancient temple on Grand Monk Mountain, built in the days before Taoism, as I meditated in front of the dragon they say lives in the cave the temple compound is built around, I went way back in time to meet Peking Man and eat Peking Duck in front of a cave somewhere between what is now Dalian and Beijing.

We sat in the new temple and we meditated, listening to the sound of the water fall. It took me back to the time before Taoism. We sat in the first temple in the area and we told stories. We prayed that the wooly mammoths would leave us alone, that they would not trample us to death, or spear us with their long tusks of ivory.

We heard stories from travellers about a great civilization in a place called Egypt, in a continent called Africa, on the other side of Asia, so far away it would take a lifetime to walk there. We heard the Egyptians had other forms of transportation, in addition to boats and beasts of burden, including camels, elephants, and horses. We heard the Egyptians came from other planets and traveled to other planets and they also traveled through time.

We thought those stories were fantastic, incredible, unbelievable.

Nobody could travel on a wooly mammoth!

The last mainland population existed in the Kyttyk Peninsula of Siberia 9,650 years ago. A small population of woolly mammoths survived on St. Paul Island, Alaska, until 6,400 years ago. The last known population remained on Wrangel Island in the Arctic Ocean until 4,000 years ago

Contrary to common belief, the woolly mammoth was hardly mammoth in size. They were roughly about the size of modern African elephants. A male woolly mammoth's shoulder height was 9 to 11 feet tall and weighed around 6 tons. Its cousin the Steppe mammoth (M. trogontherii) was perhaps the largest one in the family — growing up to 13 to 15 feet tall. The ears of a woolly mammoth were shorter than the modern elephant's ears. Like their thick coat of fur, their shortened ears were an important cold-weather adaptation because it minimized frostbite and heat loss. The woolly mammoth was not the only "woolly" type of animal. The woolly rhinoceros co-existed with the woolly mammoth, walking the Earth during the Pleistocene epoch. Like the woolly mammoth, the woolly rhino adapted to the cold with a furry coat, was depicted by human ancestors in cave paintings and became extinct around the same time.   Cave paintings drawn by ice age humans show the important relationship they had with the woolly mammoths. There is also evidence of the use of bones and tusks by humans to create portable art objects, shelters, tools, furniture and even burials.

When I returned from that past life, and returned to my apartment, after leaving the Taoist temple on the mountaintop, I jumped on my computer to find out the latest information about woolly mammoths.   Today, the hunt is on for woolly mammoth tusks in the Arctic Siberia. Due to global warming, the melting permafrost has begun revealing these hidden ivory treasures for a group of local tusk-hunters to find and sell. A tusk can range from 10-13 foot in length and a top-grade mammoth tusk is worth around $400 per pound. Mammoth ivory, unlike elephant ivory, is legal.   The first fully documented woolly mammoth skeleton was discovered in 1799. It was brought to the Zoological Museum of the Zoological Institute of the Russian Academy of Science in 1806 where Wilhelm Gottlieb Tilesius put the pieces together. Basing his task off of an Indian elephant skeleton, Tilesius was successful in reconstructing the first skeleton of an extinct animal except for one error. He put the tusks in the wrong sockets, so that they curved outward instead of inward.

The coat of a woolly mammoth consisted of a "guard" of foot long hairs, and an undercoat of shorter hairs. Preserved mammoth hair looks orange in color, however researchers believe the pigment was changed because of prolonged burial in the ground.

Even a kid can discover a preserved mammoth. In September 2012 in Russia, an 11-year-old boy named Yevgeny "Zhenya" Salinder happened upon an extremely well-preserved woolly mammoth carcass while walking his dogs. The remains were of a 16-year-old male woolly mammoth that died about 30,000 years ago. The discovery helped scientists conclude that the large "lumps" on a mammoth's back were extra stores of fat to help it survive winters. The mammoth was nicknamed "Zhenya."   The final resting place of woolly mammoths was Wrangel Island in the Arctic. Although, most of the woolly mammoth population died out by 10,000 years ago, a small population of 500-1000 woolly mammoths lived on Wrangel Island until 1650 BC. That's only about 4,000 years ago! For context, Egyptian pharoahs were midway through their empire and it was about

1000 years after the Giza pyramids were built. The reason for the demise of these woolly mammoths are unknown.

Europeans have elaborate belief systems that explain early man's discovery and use of fire. For some unknown reason, Prometheus is popular in China, unlike most other old gods popularized in the West.

Making fire with flint stones led to the Flinstones TV show, but those stones were not found in the limestone lands of China. Cavemen in China used wood. They did not rub two sticks together, they created a tool known as a fire drill.

When I went back in time to visit Peking Man, it was difficult for me to use the fire drill, the way my caveman buddies did it. They placed a stick on a flat piece of wood and made the stick spin by rubbing their hands together. That kind of friction on dry wood eventually leads to fire.

I showed them how to wrap a strip of leather, from an animal skin, around the dry stick, so they could spin it faster, with less effort, to start a fire more easily.

They thought I was a genius and treated me like a god, after that.

I told them, using grunts and pictures, that the caveman diet was very good. I tried to tell them a bit about the future and I really wanted to communicate to them the information that the paleo diet, also known as the caveman, was very popular in North America in 2014, but it was too much information and too complex for me to get across with pictograms and without words or an alphabet.

I was still learning pinyin, so I couldn't really teach them many of the symbols used in Chinese, to represent ideas with symbols. I did manage to give them the concept.

I drew a stick figure of a man and pointed to different men. They nodded their heads as though they knew that a million years ago and I was treating them like little kids. So I gave them symbols for fire and animals, as well as water and fish, fruits and vegetables, and then different types of animals, fish, fruits, and vegetables.

I wanted to tell them all about the Caveman diet.

A friend of mine, the Canadian poet Gary Barwin, got a Canada Council grant to go to Japan and teach haiku.

When I moved to China, I was asked to teach Zen meditation.

Bodhidharma took Zen to China two thousand years before me but it got lost, more or less, so I felt very good, taking Zen to China again.

I had more teaching experience than the Bodhidharma, so I didn't use his controversial methods. I didn't want any of my students to wait around for a decade and then cut his left arm off to get my attention!

Did I have to tell cavemen about the Caveman Diet?

Eat like a caveman and shed pounds: That's the theory behind the Paleo Diet.

Loren Cordain, PhD, who wrote the book on The Paleo Diet, claimed that, by eating like our prehistoric ancestors, we'll be leaner and less likely to get diabetes, heart disease, cancer, and other health problems.

I looked at my new paleo pals. Did they look like they had diabetes or other diseases? No!

It was survival of the fittest, in the most basic way. -- If you couldn't outrun an animal you hunted, and it hunted you, well, you would not live long enough to show any of the symptoms of heart disease, cancer, or other problems!

The Caveman Diet, or the Stone Age diet, is basically a high-protein, high-fiber, eating plan that promises you can lose weight without cutting calories.

My pre-historic pals ate a lot of fresh lean meat, as well as fish, fruits, and vegetables.

You can also eat eggs, nuts, and seeds.

Like a panda bear, the caveman eats shoots and leaves.

You can't eat any processed foods on this diet, but that was not a problem in the days before recorded history.

I had no idea what year it was.

Our ancestors -- the guys I met -- were hunter-gatherers, not farmers, so there was no wheat or dairy products, just wild rice and some peanuts and beans.

On the other hand, there was no refined sugar or salt, or that deadly combination that causes an epidemic of obesity in the West: salt and sugar mixed with fat and added to just about all processed foods so you feel addicted to crap that is bad for you!

There were no chocolate bars, so I missed my daily square of dark chocolate, but there was no calorie counting to worry about, either.

The fiber-rich fruits and vegetables filled me up, as well as all the lean meat.

When I lived in Ontario, I was a vegetarian, for more than half my lifetime, but when I moved to Alberta, I became a carnivore, again. When I moved to China, I ate Western foods for the first month or two but then I learned to love the local food and ate the way Chinese people in Dalian do, with fish and seafood, as well as seaweed, as well as jiaowza and jian bing.

How I missed the street food of Kaifaqu in 2014 when I was in prehistoric Peking!

Hunting and cooking took up most of our time. You need to stock up on food and cook from scratch, if you are a caveman.

There were no pre-packaged foods or meals, of course. None. Processed foods did not exist.

Exercise was not required when you're going hunting every day of your life.

I would be losing weight fast -- I could see that.

But Cordain strongly recommends weight loss for overall health and says the caveman diet is the way to do it.

I did not meet any vegetarians or vegans. Pardon the pun!

The caveman diet emphasizes meat and fish, and Cordain says it's impossible to follow a Paleo Diet without eating meat, seafood, or eggs. Excellent vegetarian sources of protein, such as beans and other legumes, are not allowed.

The diet doesn't allow salt, either, but we didn't have sodium to worry about.

If you do not eat any foods that come from a can or a box, you do not need to check the sodium on food labels.

Eating a lot of meat and fish can raise your grocery bill, but if you live in an era when money has not been invented, you don't have to worry about that.

Imagine hunting and fishing every day.

It was like living the dream shared by my male students and many of the men I met in Cold Lake, Alberta!

But what about eating duck?

And duck heads!

I talked my paleolithic pals into letting me cook a duck.

They just roasted a plucked duck on a spit.

I showed them how to blow air under the skin to separate it from the fat, then brush the duck with spices, soak it in boiling water, and hang it to dry for a day before roasting the duck.

That way, you get crispy skin and a lot less fat.

I let them have the duck heads.

In Kafaqu, Dalian, and across China, no doubt, you can see duck heads for sale in little take-out restaurants on every downtown street, but eat duck heads is still on my list of things to do. It's not high on my bucket list, but I intend to try it sometime.

Anyway, the contemporary Chinese custom of eating duck heads and not wasting any part of any plant or animal was not an issue in prehistoric times in Dongbei, or north-east China. We had mammoth meals!

Woolly mammoth meals, that is.

Oh, those mammoth steaks!

When I returned from my little visit to caveman times, I remembered watching a TV show called It's About Time, when I was a kid, and getting attached to the story about two astronauts accidentally travel back in time to prehistoric Earth. Unable to return, they make friends with the "natives", including Shad, played by Imogene Coca.

I was crazy about her.

I liked the cavemen, Gronk, Mlor, Breer, Boss, and Clon, a bit, but I really liked the cave-woman, Shad.

After chillin' with my paleolithic pals, I started looking around for a Shad of my own, of course.

I thought of the women I knew from the life I had left, or the life I lived in the 20th and 21st centuries. -- Which one of them was most like a cave-woman?

Which one of them would a cave-woman remind me of the most?

Cynthia? Harlow? Golda? Batsheva? Sherry? Cindy? Jacqui? Sue Lynn?

No!

It was Regina, the woman named after the capital city of Saskatchewan, the tall one who could do a wicked impression of Jane Hathaway, Mr. Mooney's secretary on The Beverley Hillbillies. Nancy Kulp. The woman I called The Kierkegaard Of Kifaqu.

Like Kulp, Regina was a linguist and a teacher. She was also a wannabe actress.

Shortly after I met her, the first week, she said, Want to go to Beijing this weekend? See the Forbidden City?

Or how about Kaifaqu? she said.

I wrote a book about her, but it's not going to be made available to the public for a long time, if you know what I mean.

She was a tall Canadian woman, almost six feet, with Scandinavian ancestors, from Norway and Denmark.

She had a little bit of Imogene Coca in her, too.

I looked around, half expecting to see a prehistoric version of the wildly intelligent woman, waiting for me, with that look in her eye.

When was hypomania invented? Were cavewomen liberated, or oppressed? Leaders or followers? Hunters or gatherers? Cooks or politicians? Happy or sad? Ecstatic or depressed?

Regina was hypomanic when I met her. She taught me the word and the meaning of the word and then said my problem was that I am permanently hypomanic.

Who else would want to write one hundred books set in the East after writing one hundred books in the West? she said.

She wasn't wild about China, the way I was, but I still thought she had a strong connection to Asia, going back thousands of years to our ancestors in the paleolithic period.

I was shocked when I saw a tall man with reddish hair looking at me in that way that makes women excited or nervous.

It was not until that moment that I looked down at the ground to see my feet and get a few clues as to who I was. Usually, the first thing you do when you land in a past life is look for information about your identity. When I met up with the cavemen, I just joined in, became one of the gang, did not worry about how old or young I was or if I was rich or poor or a man or ....

I was a stone age woman!

What happened next will be described in another novel that will not be made public for a long time, until I am old and grey, or long gone!

Gronk took one long look at me and I had the oddest feeling. Suddenly I had a different understanding of the phrase "done like dinner".

It was long before the development of Taoist bedroom arts or the Kama Sutra or anangaranga, of course, never mind satin sheets or soft music.

Ananga! Gronk said, Ranga!

I had no idea what the words meant, or the guttaral sounds emanating from his big mouth, but he made his intentions clear to me and the rest of our little prehistoric community.

The other men moved off.

It was like a scene out of The Clan Of The Cave Bear, after that, and I had the Darryl Hannah role.

Forget Quest For Fire! In The Clan Of The Cave Bear, a group of Neanderthal people, the "Clan", whose cave was destroyed in the earthquake and who are searching for a new home. The medicine woman of the group, Iza, discovers the girl and asks permission from Brun, the head of the Clan, to help the ailing child, despite the child being clearly a member of "the Others", the distrusted antagonists of the Clan. The child is adopted by Iza and her brother Creb. Creb is this group's "Mog-ur" or shaman, despite being deformed as a result of the difficult birth resulting from his abnormally large head and the later loss of an arm and leg after being attacked by a cave bear. The clan call her Ayla, because they can't pronounce her name. Immediately after Iza begins to help her, the clan discovers a huge, beautiful cave; many of the people begin to regard Ayla as lucky, especially since good fortune continues to come their way as she lives among them.

In Auel's books, the Neanderthal possess only limited vocal apparatus and rarely speak, but have a highly developed sign language. They do not laugh or even smile, and they do not cry; when Ayla weeps, Iza thinks she has an eye disease.

Ayla's different thought processes lead her to break important Clan customs, particularly the taboo against females handling weapons. She is self-willed and spirited, but tries hard to fit in with the Neanderthals, although she has to learn everything first-hand; she does not possess the ancestral memories of the Clan which enable them to do certain tasks after being shown only once.

Her main antagonist is Broud, son of the leader, an egomaniac who feels that she takes credit and attention away from him. As the two mature, the hatred between them festers. When they are young adults, Broud rapes Ayla, but she becomes pregnant, and rejoices in the birth of a son.

Gronk knew nothing about love or lovemaking or anything except rape .... Until he met me.

Gronk said, "Hi there! Want to go to Peking? The Forbidden City? The Palace Of Heaven? Right now?!"

Of course, I had no idea what Gronk said, because I didn't speak Cave-man, but I had a strong feeling that he was saying the Stone Age equivalent of, "Live around here often?"

I knew that line -- "Want to go to Beijing for the weekend? -- from 2013. A certain hypomanic woman used that line on me.

I thought she was crazy, or might be, so I talked her into going to a movie at the new Imax in Dalian, instead.

We saw Gravity, with Sandra Bullock, floating in space, from every conceivable angle, and George Cluney acting like Buzz Lightyear, showing how far man had not evolved from the the Stone Age days.

In retrospect, I wished I had said "Yes" to that invitation to Beijing, to see The Forbidden City and the Temple Of Heaven, not to mention eating Peking duck in the city we used to call Peking, not to mention duck tongue.

Remembering all that changed my perspective on Gronk, a bit. He looked different, all of a sudden. He started to resemble a panda bear, I thought, and I remembered my favourite grammer book from the 2000s: Eats, Shoots, And Leaves. -- It had a picture of a panda bear on the front cover.

Needless to say, Gronk knew nothing about Taoist Tantra, since philosophy hadn't been invented, yet.

He couldn't even count to six, or eight, or nine, until I taught him, and he knew nothing about yin and yang, until I showed him.

It was Gronk who gave me my prehistoric name. It sounded like three grunts, to me, but he made it clear, with the use of pictures, pointing, and pantomine, that he wanted my name to be White Tigress.

"Oh, Gronk," I said. "You flatter me!"

He took me by the hand and showed me a sbre toothed tiger, in the wild, that had white fur with black stripes, instead of yeallow, and was obviously a female, as she had a tiger cub with her.

Gronk did not look hapy, the first time I saw him, or the last, but he had the look of prehistoric happiness or Stone Age ecstasy for a little while, when we were together.

What can I say? I was a cavewoman!

"Nice cave, Gronk," I said. "Decorate this place yourself?"

He had the skins of several animals on the dirt floor and rock walls.

The rest of the clan wanted me to make roast duck for them, again, but I let them know I had to go.

I did not even try to tell them I was going back to the future.

I thought of trying to bring Gronk with me.

Or Bonk, as I came to call him.

If I could teach that caveman how to scate and play hockey, I felt fairly certain he could crack the line-up of the Edmonton Oilers, or at least the Dalian Ice Dragons, as a stay-at-home, defensive defenceman. After a few seasons, he might make it with the Chicago Blackhawks, and he could play with the aboriginal person's head crest on his chest and the crossed stone age hammers on his shoulders.

.

Chapter 5. Zen Santa

One of the biggest surprises I got on my first and every day in China was the sight of The Laughing Buddha just about everywhere I looked.

When I lived in the West, I got the impression that Buddha, the Laughing Buddha, and Buddhism belonged to the past, in China, but I was completely wrong about that.

I was happy to be wrong about that!

The first car that came along, to pick me up, at the airport, had a Laughing Buddha statue on the dashboard. The car in front of it and the car behind it had Laughing Buddhas attached to their dashboards, too.

I looked at all the cars passing by, on the highway, and it looked as though most of them had Laughing Buddhas on their dashboards.

The city of Dalian, with a population of six million, at least, and counting, as the place is growing fast, had around six million cars. That's the way it looked.

There must have been at least a million Laughing Buddhas out there.

What about the restaurants?

As I discovered more and more restaurants, I found more and more Laughing Buddhas.

I wrote a book about the Laughing Buddha, called Santa Claus And The Laughing Buddha, and I've rubbed the bellies of a million Laughing Buddhas, over the years.

At work, I found out the students called me The Christmas Man, meaning Santa Claus, or Mr. KFC, but not The Laughing Buddha.

Why? I asked.

Well, one kid said, "You foreign teacher guys, the white men, Caucasians, all look alike to us, and you look like the white guys we see on TV, so ...."

"Also," he added, "we really like KFC!"

That saved it, for me.

Next year at Hallowe'en, I plan to wear a white suit with a string tie and let my goatee grow in white, so I look even more like Colonel Sanders.

I heard that our school superintendent, a former hockey star with Canada's national team, who had a bit of a belly, in his final year of retirement, sometimes had the strange experience of having strange Chinese people walk up to him and rub his belly, out of the blue, which made him feel strange, until somebody told him they were doing it for good luck and it was a great compliment to be connected to The Laughing Buddha like that.

So, to make a long story a little shorter, it came as no surprise to me that when I did some Past Life work, I went back in time to the period when The Laughing Buddha was around.

How did Buddha become to fat and jolly? you ask.

Doesn't that seem unlikely for a spiritual guy from India in that era?

When most westerners think of "Buddha," they don't usually visualize the Buddha of history, meditating or teaching, they generally visualize a fat, bald, jolly character called "The Laughing Buddha."

That guy you see, smiling away, beside cash registers in Chinese restaurants all over the place.

Where did that guy come from?

The Laughing Buddha emerged from Chinese folktales of the 10th century, and that was where, or when, I found myself. The 900s.

The original stories of the Laughing Buddha centered on a Ch'an, or Zen, monk named Ch'i-t'zu, or Qieci, from Fenghua, in what is now the province of Zhejiang.

Ch'i-t'zu was an eccentric but much-loved character who worked small wonders such as predicting the weather.

hejiang, formerly romanized as Chekiang or Che-Keang, is an eastern coastal province of the People's Republic of China. The word Zhejiang means zigzagging river.

When I found myself on the shore of Thousand Islets Lake in the 10th Century, I expected to experience something special.

Thousand Islets Lake, or Qian Dao Lake, is a pure lake with clean, fresh air, in the forest.

It is a young lake, formed in 1959, as a result of the construction of New Anjiang Hydroelectric Power Station.

It is a beautiful lake with over a thousand little islands that reminded me of the Thousand Islands area of Ontario, which is on the border between Canada and the U.S.A. near Don Cherry's favourite little city, Kingston, and the town of Ganonoque.

Both lakes have a lot of fish and are in the forest.

The trees in Canada are mostly maples and white pines and in China they are tea trees and mulberry, the food of the silkworm, as well as fruit trees.

Qian Dao Lake and the St. Laurence River both feature is also many activities aimed at enjoying the natural scenery and local culture, observing wild animals and taking part in many exciting activities, such as kayaking and power boating.

Thousand Islets Lake, or Qian Dao Lake, lies in Chun'an County, about 150 km (93 miles) west of Hangzhou City and is 140 km (87 miles) southeast of Mt. Huangshan.

They call it a resplendent pearl in the classical golden route of Hangzhou-Thousand Islets Lake-Mt. Huangshan and claim it has become popular all over the world.

Qian Dao Lake is noted for its verdurous mountains, crystal clear water, exotic caves, and strange stones.

Nongfu (farmer) Spring Water, a famous mineral water brand, comes from Qiandao Lake.

The scenic area can be divided into six sections on the basis of geographical location. They are: Southeast Lake District (the first to be developed), Central Lake District (combining several spots that should not be missed), Southwest Lake District, Northeast Lake District, Northwest Lake District and Fuxi Stone Forest (the first stone forest in East China), each possessing their own unique and striking landscapes.

Qiandao Lake in HangzhouIn Southeast Lake District can be found Tianchi (heaven pool), a quarry site dating from the Southern Song Dynasty (1127-1279), Xianshan (admiration mountain) Island, Guihua (sweet osmanthus) Island and Mishan (honey mountain) Island (The story of 'One boy is a boy, two boys half a boy, three boys no boy' originated here).

In Central Lake District, there are Qiandao Lake Fishing Village, Meifeng (plum peak) Island, Wulong (five dragons) Scenic Area and the Animal Interest Section.

On Meifeng Island, you can command views from a great height, experience grass-skiing, and boat down the water.

Wulong Scenic Area is made up of Lock Island, Bird Island, Zhenqu (true delight) Garden and Qishi (strange stone) Island connected by several bridges.

Lock Island is a world of locks, including happiness lock, wisdom lock, health lock and carp lock.

The first Lock Museum in China was built here housing Safety Lock, the biggest lock in Guinness World Records.

In the Animal Interest Section, peacocks, snakes, monkeys, and ostriches can be seen.

You can watch the animals performing, feed them, play with them, and take photos of them.

The best time to visit Qiandao Lake, they say, is in autumn and winter, when there is less rainfall, and the weather is cool, with fresh air.

Distinctively cooked seafood and some local food is popular here.   Souvenirs from the region include inkstones, hemp embroideries, and products made of pearls.

Thousand Islets Lake is the largest forest park in China. It has been awarded many titles and received favorable comments from tourists both at home and abroad.

Gananoque, Ontario, Canada in the heart of the Thousand Islands on the other side of the planet.   It features camping, kayaking, a Charity Casino, and lots of hotels motels, cottages and restaurants.

This part of the St. Lawrence River is easy to enter from New York State via the Thousand Island International Bridge.   Gananoque is the nearest town, 16 km (10 mi) west, from the Thousand Islands International Bridge.

Gananoque has a population of just 5, 209 peple.

It is 288 km (179 mi) east of Toronto, , 272 km (169 mi) west of Montreal, 167 km (104 mi) South of Ottawa, 16 km (10 mi) west of the 1000 Islands Bridge to the U.S.A., just and minutes to Kingston or Brockville.

I knew, going in, that, according to tradition, just before Ch'i-t'zu died, he revealed himself to be an incarnation of Maitreya Buddha.

Maitreya is the Buddha of a future age.

Ch'i-t'zu's last words were:

Maitreya, true Maitreya Reborn innumerable times From time to time manifested among men The men of the age do not recognize him.

The tales of Ch'i-t'zu spread throughout China, and he came to be called Pu-tai (Budai), which means "hempen sack."

When I opened my eyes in the Lake District in the 900s, I made eye contact with a guy who looked as though he knew me and when I asked him about The Laughing Buddha, he told me the whole story: "He carries a sack with him full of good things, such as sweets for children, and he is often pictured with children," he said. "Pu-tai represents happiness, generosity and wealth, and he is a protector of children as well as of the poor and the weak."

The tradition of rubbing Pu-tai's belly for good luck is a folk practice, however, not a Buddhist teaching.

Pu-tai also is associated with the last panel of the Ten Ox-herding Pictures. These are ten images that represent stages of enlightenment in Ch'an (Zen) Buddhism.

The last panel shows an enlightened master who enters towns and marketplaces to give ordinary people the blessings of enlightenment.

Pu-tai followed the spread of Buddhism into other parts of Asia, outside of China.

In Japan he became one of the Seven Lucky Gods of Shinto and is called Hotei.

He also was incorporated into Chinese Taoism as a deity of abundance.

Hotei is most likely based on the itinerant 10th-century Chinese Buddhist monk and hermit Budaishi (d. 917), who is said to be an incarnation of Miroku Bodhisattva (Maitreya in Sanskrit).

Hotei is sometimes shown surrounded by a group of small children, romping and squealing in delight around his rotund shape. In recent times, Hotei is also referred to as the patron saint of restaurateurs and bartenders. When one over eats and over drinks, one may sometimes jokingly attribute it to Hotei's influence.

Hotei is a semi-legendary itinerant 10th-century Buddhist monk who became a popular subject in Chinese and Japanese ink painting. His real name is said to have been Qici (Keishi), whose biography is found in the 908 Song Gaosenzhuan or the "Legends of High Priests of the Song Dynasty." He lived on Mt. Siming in Mingzhou, Fenghua, where he frequently strolled through a nearby town carrying his large cloth bag.

Budai's air of "enlightened innocence" led him, like Hanshan and Shide Kanzan Jittoku, to be admired as an exemplar of Zen values.

Although originally he was said to have filled his bag with anything he encountered on his wanderings, later Zen interpretations speak of Budai's "empty bag."

Ironically, in Japanese popular culture Budai's bulging bag and contented appearance led to his inclusion in the Seven Gods of Good Fortune.

In paintings, Budai is shown with sparse hair, a smiling face, a large bare belly, loose garments and carrying a bag and wooden staff. In later paintings he is shown in a variety of poses, usually seated or sleeping on his bag, but also dancing, walking or pointing upwards at the moon. In Edo period painting Budai is frequently pictured together with groups of playing children. Early Chinese examples include paintings by Liang Kai.

Hotei could be the Chinese hermit Budaishi (d. 917), who was thought to be an incarnation of Maitreya; the latter is venerated in some Zen monasteries of the Oubaku sect by the name of Hotei, the "Miroku with the Large Belly."

He is represented as a Buddhist monk: bald, unshaven, smiling, with a huge belly. He holds a non-folding fan in the right hand, and leans on a large sack which contains endless treasures, a sort of horn of plenty for his followers.

He is also sometimes confused with Warai-Hotoke (smiling Buddha) or with Fudaishi (Japanese version of the name of the Chinese hermit Budaishi) when he is assigned to guard monastery libraries.

In this case he is accompanied by his two "sons".

In Japan, the image of Hotei is often made as a toy for pulling or tilting. When it has wheels, the toy is called kuruma-sou (the rolling monk). In some representations in Japan, Hotei has an eye drawn on his back, a symbol of universal vision.

A legend relates, against all the evidence, that Fudaishi was the inventor of the buildings intended to contain the sutras (rotating libraries, called kyōdō in Japan), and built by the so-called Azekura-zukuri technique.

His two sons, shown clapping their hands and laughing, are sometimes called Fuwaku (or Fuken) and Fukon (or Fujō).

Sculptures at Kōmyō-ji Temple in Kamakura, and at Daikoku-ji Temple in Kyōto. Hotei. In Chinese folklore he's an eccentric Zen monk and the epitome of contentment. His name means "cloth sack," because he carries all his belongings in a bindle wherever he goes. He also stuffs the sack with donations of food and clothing from laymen, and candy to give to children — a veritable fat, jolly, Asian Santa Claus. In this picture, Hotei himself is in his bag — and some have noted that the bag is a kind of ensō or Zen circle symbolizing Enlightenment, non-duality, and/or emptiness. Non-Buddhist Westerners often confuse Hotei with the historical Buddha, and the Chinese themselves sometimes refer to him as The Laughing Buddha. Some believe he is an earthly manifestation of the bodhisattva Maitreya. Legend has it that when Hotei died, he recited the following verse:

Maitreya, the true Maitreya

Has billions of incarnations.

Often he is shown to people at the time;

Other times they do not recognize him.

Hotei also serves duty as one of the Japanese Seven Gods of Good Fortune — the god of abundance and good health.

That's a lot of weight for that happy little guy to carry in his bindle!

There's a Zen story about Hotei. When asked "What's the significance of Zen?" he put his sack down on the ground. When then asked "What's the actualization of Zen?" he picked his sack back up and walked away. Clever Hotei! The very essence of Zen — letting go and dropping off whatever we're holding. The very actualization of Zen — drawing water and chopping wood. Hotei lives life at the crosshairs of the Absolute and the Relative. A lot like Hakuin himself.

When Hotei was not busy being all these things, he served double duty as Hakuin's alter-ego and his Everyman. While Hakuin's Hotei is a spiritual fellow and sits zazen, he also enjoys the pleasures of secular life. In painting after painting we see him puffing on a pipe (and what comes out of the pipe is not a smoke ring, but the prostitute Otufuko!), flying up in the air as a kite, playing go, riding a colt, playing kickball, and street juggling.

There's a remarkable resemblance between Hotei and Santa -- both fat and jolly, both carry bags of good things for children, both somewhat magical.

Both characters represent happiness, generosity and abundance and are especially associated with children, so they could be interchangeable -- albeit in different costumes, and one has a full beard and hair and the other doesn't.

Saint Nicholas -- from whose life the original "Santa Claus" legend slowly emerged -- was a 4th century Christian bishop, and Ch'i-t'zu -- the Ch'an monk of Zhejiang, China, who was the original "laughing buddha" -- probably lived in the 10th century. But Hotei (or Pu-Tai in China) has been fat, jolly, and sack-carrying for centuries, whereas Santa Claus didn't take on these attributes until the 19th century. How did that happen?

According to Kelli Mahoney, About.com Guide to Christian Teens, today's iconic Santa Claus was a collaboration between Clement Clarke Moore, an Episcopal Minister, and Thomas Nast, a cartoonist. In 1822 Moore wrote An Account of a Visit from St. Nicholas, better known as 'Twas the Night Before Christmas. In this poem Santa became a "fat, jolly old elf" with a bagful of toys. Illustrations for the poem drawn by Thomas Nast in 1881 filled in the white beard and red suit, which Santa has worn ever since.

Before Moore, the various depictions of Saint Nicholas or Father Christmas were less jolly and corpulent, although in some parts of Europe he had carried a bag for a while. But there wasn't much resemblance to Hotei until Moore got hold of Santa.
I understand that Moore never traveled in Asia. In 1822 he was working as a professor of Greek and Oriental literature, but "Oriental" in those days referred to what we would call the "Middle East" today, not China or Japan.

However, in 1822 there was a small Chinese community in Manhattan, where Moore lived and worked. Chinese sailors and traders began coming to New York in the 18th century, and some stayed in New York, married, and raised families. So it is not impossible that Moore had seen depictions of the Laughing Buddha and was subliminally influenced by them when he imagined his jolly Santa Claus.

However, I think it's more likely they came to resemble each other because they filled the same niche in their respective cultures. Happiness, generosity, abundance and children are valued everywhere.

In all the Past Life work I've done, I've usually seen myself as someone close to somebody famous, such as Norman Bethune, Marco Polo, Bodhidarma, or a Chinese emperor, but whenever I thought about The Laughing Buddha or whenever I do Past Life work aimed at his era, I get the impression, quite powerfully, that I was, in fact, Put Tai, the big guy, himself.

Maybe it's because I had a big belly, for a few years, I'm losing m hair, and I'm happy, even ecstatic, so much of the time that people often ask me, "What's your secret?"
I've been nominated for the Stephen Leacock Award For Humour three or four times.

I laugh a lot. I'm writing a book about happiness. My working titles include The Tao Of Bliss, Ecstasy Every Day, and How To Be Joyful. My Zen master buddy wants to do a book with me called How To Die Happy.

I've always liked the Laughing Buddha.

A few years ago, I wrote a book called Santa Claus And The Laughing Buddha. I walked along the beach at JinShiTan, my feet in the Yellow Sea, my eyes on the Black Mountains, feeling happy with the warm water, the air, the beach, but when I looked down to see my feet, after walking into the past, I saw the yellow skin of a big guy's big feet, so I wondered if I was a suomo wrestler in the era when those guys performed for different monasteries in China.

I wrestled in high school, one year, but I was lean and mean, in those days, built like a hockey player, not a super-sized wrestler. Those big suomo guys in their loincloths always made me laugh.

My favourite big Buddhist wrester was the white guy in the American movie called Anger Management, with Jack Nicholson and Adam Sandler teaming up to get even with an old school yard bully, decades later, who has become a Buddhist but looks like a suomo wrestler.

My big feet, magnified a bit by the water, made me laugh. They looked like clown feet. I could not help but notice that my belly shook, when I laughed, like a bowl full of jelly.

I was an Oriental St. Nick, a Santa Claus of the Far East.

I spoke Chinese and wore a light robe in a hot climate, not a red suit at the North Pole.

In truth, I identify more with the North Pole than the tropics. But in this life I was, apparently, a big guy in a hot part of China.

Lucky for me, there was a big lake nearby with spring water so fresh you could drink it straight up, to cool down.

My belongings were in a burlap bag. Or was that hemp?

I wished I had a hot drink, to cool me off, it was such a hot day, so I reached into my hemp bag and pulled out a little container of tea, almost too hot to drink.

I was like the Sai Baba, I realized: I could reach into that bag and pull out whatever you wanted.

In the 2000s, I had a friend who wrote the Findhorn Book of Abundancy, namely Karen Hood-Caddy, and I studied with a New Age guru named Janet Amare who travelled the world to work with the great healers alive on the planet at that time, including John of God and, a decade before he died, the Sai Baba.

They say the Sai Baba, as a kid, could sit under a fruit tree and make his friends happy by pulling any and every kind of fruit they wanted to eat out of that one tree.

That was the trick I did for kids, using my hemp bag.

Then, as in 2014, I was a Zen guy, but I did not follow the path called Forest Zen, in the 900s, I just lived in the forest and I loved Zen.

I was famous for my laughter, my belly, and my bag of tricks.

Sometimes big Buddhist scholars who would find me in the forest and ask me skill-testing questions about Buddhism. "What is Zen?" they would say.

I would just drop my big bag.

"How do you practice Zen?" they asked me again and again.

I'd pick up my bag, again, and walk away, doing my thing, manifesting magical things for children and other people.

To this day, Hotei is called the god of contentment and happiness, guardian of children, and patron of bartenders. Hotei has a cheerful face and a big belly. He is supposedly based on an actual person, and is widely recognized outside of Japan as the Fat, Laughing Buddha. He carries a large cloth bag over his back, one that never empties, for he uses it to feed the poor and needy. It includes an inexhaustible cache of treasures, including food and drink.

Chapter 6: I Was A Chinese Woman

"Often the object of a desire, when desire is transformed into hope, becomes more real than reality itself," Umberto Eco observed in his magnificent atlas of imaginary places, The Book Of Legendary Lands.

That might explain my relationship with Regina .

She reminded me of Ishtar, the ancient goddess of love and war and sex and fertility. Ishtar, pronounced Easter, was originally the celebration of the Assyrian and Babylonian goddess of fertility and sex. Her symbols were eggs and bunnies, representing fertility and sex.

I had a strong feeling that I was connected to this woman in this life and previous lives.

Her name is Regina. We met in China shortly after I arrived. She had been here for over a year. We hit it off quickly. It was almost like love at first sight. But we aren't kids, like Romeo and Juliet. We both said we felt we had been connected for a long time. She told me that she said, to herself, "So that's what he looks like," when she saw me for the first time. I told her I had the same sort of feeling of recognition.

I felt as though I had found my other half and I was surprised to find her in China, on the other side of the planet from where I was born and spent most of my life. She said she did not believe in past lives, past life work, reincarnation, or "any of that crap", to use her words.

I told her I had a certificate in past life work and she did not run away.

When we first got together, everything went so well that she proposed, suggested living together, planned our future lives together, and I thought we were on our way to a Hollywood ending, living happily ever after.

Not everyone believes in past lives, of course; not even my friends believe in it, even after I do past life work with them.

That doesn't matter to me.

If someone has a point of view I find difficult to understand or appreciate, I use another little trick, or technique, to help me see things through their eyes.

What you do is, with their permission, imagine and visualize that you are entering into the person's body, through their third eye, and sitting inside, so you get a sense of their mind and emotions.

I tried that with a friend of mine, to find out what she thought of me and my work in the area of past lives. And here's how it went:

"What are you going on about now?" I said.

I He gave me a long lecture on Jing, Chi, and Shen:

Jing, Chi and Shen are the 3 types of internal energy which are cultivated and utilized in martial arts practice.

Jing, sometimes given in English as Ching, is the densest and most material of the three. In Taoist teachings Jing is associated with sexual energy and is cultivated in sexual practices such as those of the Jade Dragon and White Tigress teachings. In this sense it is somewhat similar to the western psychological term 'libido' as it is used in the work of Carl Jung to refer not only to sexual desire but more generally to describe the psychic energy of the subconscious mind. Recognizing the unity of mind and matter Jung said that below the level of the subconscious mind there is a level of reality which is neither mind nor matter but reconciles these two nature into one. Jing may be thought of as existing at this point where mind meets matter.

Chi, or Qi, is the most widely known of the internal energies. But despite this it is perhaps the most difficult to describe or analyse. Chi is more refined and etheral than Jing, but less so than Shen. Chi is stored within the 'Dan Tien' whic resides in the centre of the torso about two inches below the level of the navel and can be drawn from this source to be used. All 3 kinds of energy are connected and work together, and being in the middle of the three Chi is often used as a convenient description for phenomena which involve all three. Perhaps the best way to conceptualize Chi is to describe it according to its effects - a sense of vitality and vigour, positivity and joy.

Shen is the highest and most rarified of the three. It can be literally translated as 'mind' but what would be referred to as the power of Shen is very different from that which a westerner may consider to be the power of mind. In may ways the eastern concept of mind described by Shen is closer to western ideas of spirit than to the psychological concept of mind. When a westerner talks about the mind they most often refer to the contents or processes of mind - thought, logic, feelings and so on. Shen does not refer to the contents of mind but rather to the underlying reality of 'pure mind'. It may be more accurately translated as 'attention' or 'awareness' instead of 'mind', although something of its nature would still be lost in translation.

It is said that Shen leads the Chi which leads the Jing, and that Jing may be refined and transformed into Chi which can be transformed into Shen during the course of spiritual development.

Of course, I told him I thought Chi was a bunch of New Age nonsense, or Buddhist bullshit, and I had never heard of Jing and Shen.

Patience, Grasshopper, he said, alluding to a TV show called Kung Fu. It was a line said, famously, to the star, Kwai Chang Caine, by one of his Shaolin teachers, he told me. The teacher asked Kwai Chang how is it he didn't hear the grasshopper at his feet. Kwai Chang asked his teacher how is it that he DID hear the grasshopper. After that, the teacher called Kwai Chang "Grasshopper" to remind him of that lesson.

"If you can do that," I told him, "Well, then .... I've hit the jackpot."

Not only did it feel like a full body massage, it felt fantastic!

He told me that in addition to being a Reiki master and Zen meditation teacher, a certified qigong instructor with a diploma in energy healing, he had learned a lot about reflexology and how to make a foot massage feel like a full body massage.

No way! I said.

He smiled and nodded.

Oh, alright, I said. Sock on or sock off? I asked, as I took off my socks.

While he rubbed my feet, one after the other, I told him my whole life story, about my family of origin, my parents, running away at age 14, missing most of high school, going to university as a mature student, doing extremely well at school, despite missing high school, and how I had no interest in dating or men for years and years. After my divorce and the death of my ex-husband, I nursed my mother through the death process, and then I had a falling out with my brother. I raised my kids and launched them into the world. It was only recently that I decided to live for myself, after decades of focusing on my kids and I now wanted to be independent and free.

He nodded his head and said he understood.

He told me to sit back and relax and he would tell me something else about himself that would convince me he understood.

Yeah, right, I said to myself. He just wants to take advantage of me.

He told my about working with a New Age guru and learning a lot about past lives as well as becoming a Reiki master and getting a diploma in energy healing.

I don't believe in all that past life nonsense, I said. Isn't it just a metaphor?

That's the way we were taught to look at it, he said. But it feels so real, a lot of people feel moved to do some historical research, which tends to confirm what they learned about their past lives.

I still don't believe it, I said.

Before he did it, he thought it was nothing but nonsense, too, he said.

You've done past life work?

Lots of it, he said. For other people and for myself.

"So you think we met in a past life?" I said, rolling my eyes.

"How else would you explain our connection and comfort, the way we get along, how well things go when we're together, how much we have in common, how it feels we've been married for a long time, already, even though we just met, really, and have spent a few days together.

I nodded my head.

He told me he wrote a book about it, set in Alberta, called In Love And War, that covered five hundred years in three hundred and sixty five pages, about a couple that finds each other in life after life, starting out with two people who are First Nations Aboriginal Canadian people and going through a lot of lives as white people and then turning into a Chinese couple, as the women of China rose up and took over Canada and the world. Sounds good, I said, and not that unlikely.

In each era, they recognize each other more easily, he said. They say things like, Oh, there you are. I've been looking for you.

I nodded my head.

So, there you are, he said. I've been looking for you.

I don't believe in that sort of crap, I told him.

But when we met, you said, "So that's what he looks like".

Well, I said, I don't know where that came from. It was just a thought that popped into my head.

He said, I have a feeling we were together in a previous life. And maybe you were the man and I was the woman. And we must have some unfinished business. That's why we had to meet again in this lifetime in this place.

We had to meet in China? I said. I don't think so.

I have a feeling that our past life, or past lives, were in China.

We were Chinese, I said, sounding skeptical.

He changed the subject.

How would you like a neck and shoulder rub?

I don't know about that, I said. Rubbing that could lead to rubbing other things and then I'd be in trouble.

But then I added, Okay. But just my neck and shoulders.

I moved from the couch to sit on a chair so he could sit behind my and I lowered whatever the hell I was wearing so he could have access to my skin. I pulled my hair up and pinned it to the top of my head so my long neck and smooth skin was revealed.

Your skin! he said. It's so smooth and silky!

"It's the Silk Road!" I giggled.

He showed me how drama people do a type of massage that involves finding knots in the muscles of the shoulders. He found a knot and pressed on it until it let go, dissolved, disappeared.

I liked that, I said.

You have big strong hands, I said. That's good.

He massaged me softly and then a little more firmly. His hands enjoyed my soft skin, he told me, and he said I looked beautiful from behind, with my hair up.

His fingers traced my breast bone, which was quite long, he said, and he told me it was beautiful, too.

I relaxed into the massage for several minutes but then jumped up.

Okay, I said. That's it. One minute more and I won't be able to leave.

I said the same thing when we hugged goodbye at the door.

She took me out to lunch the day after I did the past life work and I told her that I saw her but it didn't feel real. We went to the Pizza Hut in Jinshitan Station. She laughed in my face.

That past life crap is such bullshit! she said.

She also told me that she loved me.

She has trouble saying things like that, so she didn't actually say the words, but she did say it, in her fashion. She said, Sometimes I hate you.

We got together again two days later, on Sunday, and I took her up the mountain to the ancient Taoist temple. She was feeling unhappy when we got together but after I took her to lunch, got a driver to take us up Big Monk Mountain, freed two birds, fed the fish in the koi ponds, tied red fabric wishes to trees, got down on our knees to pray, inhaled incense, walked up and down a thousand stairs, gave money to a beggar, and she had her fortune told, she finally started to perk up

The week leading up to Easter, this year, was a tough one. The Sunday before, I took her up the mountain to the ancient Taoist temple I'd discovered in the Kaifaqu area of Dalian, in China, which was older than Taoism and Buddhism but influenced by both.

That ancient place was beautiful, she said.

I took her to a Western-style restaurant for lunch and then phoned for a driver to take us up the mountain to the Taoist temple and wait for us while we walked up and down the many stairs linking one little temple's courtyard to another on the side of the mountain.

I loved the place and loved showing her all the things I had discovered: the ponds, the fish, the turtles, the birds, the pear trees, the golden tree, the prayers or wishes written in Chinese on strips of red fabric and tied to trees, the sculptures, especially the beautiful, elaborate, colourful dragon and the lotus, at the heart of the temple compound.

Taoism is all about health and happiness, I told her, and it includes the famous Taoist bedroom arts, which describe how love and sex can be used to heal the heart and body so you live a long and happy life.

There was a spring in the temple and the water was channeled so it flowed out of the dragon's mouth to land on a sculpted lotus.

I did not have to explain the sexy symbolism to her.

She was smart but depressed and only commented on the flaws she noticed: dead fish in the coy pond, dirt and dust on the stairs, ashes in the graveyard, the captured animals sold for Taoist rituals.

I bought two birds and took the cage to stone arch overlooking a pond and invited her to lift the little door to the cage so the birds could fly to freedom, but she waved me off.

She wanted to have her fortune told by a man with cards but felt frustrated because he didn't speak English and she didn't speak Chinese.

I opened the little door to the bird cage and watched as one flew into a nearby tree and the other flew high in the sky.

Regina wandered away to explore the temple compounds linked by stone stairways on her own, so I bought a half dozen strips of red cloth with prayers or wishes written on them with Chinese characters. I offered them to her but she said, I've already prayed, in my own way.

I tied them to incense burners and wished she would find happiness. I prayed for an end to her depression. I wished her diagnosis, from the West, for a lifetime of bipolar disorder, could be healed by Traditional Chinese Medicine and Taoist bedroom arts from the West.

A few hours later, after we drove down the mountain and returned to Kaifaqu, she was feeling slightly better but I was getting depressed. As her mood lifted, mine went down.

When we parted, she said, Don't let me drag you down, destroy your joie de vivre, or zap your energy.

But it was too late.

The next day I told her that the black dog that had followed her for decades had followed me home.

She said, Kick it in the face!

I tried many things in my bag of tricks to lift my spirits: meditation, sleep, rest, exercise, work, writing, smiling, helping other people, taichi, qigung, you name it.
I lost myself in work but it didn't go so well, since I was getting depressed, and my lack of success at work had the opposite of the desired effect.

However, I got through work, got everything done, and it all turned out well, and on Thursday night I went out to dinner with a group of friends. I helped put our little outing together. It was a farewell and get well soon dinner for a friend and neighbour who was going to Thailand for throat surgery. I got one of the women in our group to bring a card she made and we asked everyone to sign it. We all walked together to a restaurant we loved and the nine of us had a good time sitting around a big round table in a small square room sharing nine different dishes, all of them delicious.

We walked to another restaurant for ice cream, after dinner, and then a few of us jumped in a cab together to go home.

It was a terrific evening, full of kind conversation from good people who wanted to do something for our friend. There was no drama, no tension, no sorrow, and no problems or worries, I noticed, in sharp contradistinction to my communication with Regina.

She had a good week, getting a little happier day by day, looking better, and laughing more.

I did some past life work to see if I could find out what had happened with us in the past that might be of some use in the present.

In ancient China, I learned, mental disorders were treated mainly under Traditional Chinese Medicine by herbs, acupuncture or "emotional therapy". The Inner Canon of the Yellow Emperor described symptoms, mechanisms and therapies for mental illness, emphasizing connections between bodily organs and emotions. Conditions were thought to comprise five stages or elements and imbalance between Yin and yang.

Chapter 7. Past Life #7: The Female Empress

The number 69 popped into my mind, but that is the number we use to represent the yin-yang symbol, and I had just walked over one in the courtyard of the temple. There was a beautiful black and white symbol before a gateway leading to a stone stairway that went up to another gateway and courtyard with a wall, where the golden tree, a beautiful pagoda, and more temples were located. So I did not take 69 as the year I would travel to. I gave my fuzzy head a shake so a different number could come in but 69 came back again and again. After several attempts, there was a zero attached to it, so I went to the year 690. Six centuries after the start of the Common Era.

That was an interesting time in China as there was a female emperor.

I knew that in the history of China, there has been more than 400 emperors, since the time the first one used the word, two hundred years before the Common Era. From 221 BCE to 1921 AD, there were hundreds of emperors in China but only one female on the list.

Imperial China lasted a long time, from the first emperor to the last, who abdicated, at the end of the Qing Dynasty. The one and only female Emperor in the history of Imperial China was known as Empress Wu Zetian.

There was no established, clear-cut, or legal way that a woman in imperial China could rise to the rank of ruler. The laws of succession prohibited woman from taking over the top position.

However, Empress Wu Zetian did the impossible. She defied all the odds and founded her own Dynasty. She was the power behind the throne, with a series of puppet emperors, who did what she told them to do, and then she ruled for 15 years.

Of China's 400 emperors, only 7 lived beyond the age of 80, and Empress Wu Zetian was one of them.

How did this woman do it?

I had a feeling I was about to find out.

After I went for a long walk along my imaginary beach, which looked like JinShiTan, or Golden Pebble Beach, along Golden Bay of the Yellow Sea, in the Greater Dalian Area, I found myself in the year 690. I looked down at the ground and found out I was standing in a white stone courtyard and I was wearing the shoes of someone who belonged in the court of the emperor.

I looked around and saw a lot of women who looked like concubines and one of them caught my eye with a knowing look. It appeared as though we were old friends. So, I asked her about our emperor.

She was born in 604, she said, and ever since she was a young girl she had a love for reading, which she developed, so she became quite knowledgeable. At the age of 14, she was chosen to be a concubine for Emperor Tang Taizong, a man old enough to be her father. He already had a lot of concubines.

How did that work out for her? I asked, asking the Dr. Phil question over fifteen hundred years ago.

She was not from the rich and powerful family, and her father passed away when she was young, my gossipy friend told me. So, she could not use family influence to get a higher ranking as a concubine. She remained a lowly concubine all the time Emperor Tang Taizong was alive, and that gave her some ideas about what to do with her life after that.

From a young age, her cold-hearted ambition was obvious to all of us, she said. There was a time when Emperor Tang Taizong had a horse nobody could tame. Wu Zetian told him she could tame the horse. All she needed, she said, was an iron whip, an iron hammer, and a sharp dagger.

She would first whip the horse with the iron whip, she said, and if the horse did not submit, she would use the hammer on its head.

If the horse was still not submissive, she would stab it with the dagger.

She would kill it, if she had to.

Emperor Tang Taizong did not like that. He was a kind man who loved animals. He said Wu Zetian was too cold-hearted and he ignored her, after that.

Wu Zetian knew that Emperor Tang Taizong did not like her so she forgot about him and targeted the crown prince, Li Zhi.

She developed a romantic relationship with the Crown Prince, my friend said. In other words, she seduced him.

After the death of Emperor Tang Taizong, all his concubines were sent to a temple to become Buddhist nuns.

That was the time that Wu Zetian's strategy paid off. The new emperor, Emperor Tang Gaozong, loved her and acted upon Empress Wang's suggestion to take Wu Zetian as his concubine.

Emperor Tang Gaozong loved Consort Xiao more than Empress Wang. Empress Wang thought that with the help of Wu Zetian, she could reduce the influence of Consort Xiao. She had chosen the wrong person to be the weapon in the war of jealousy.

Wu Zetian took steps to get rid of her "enemies" namely Empress Wang and Consort Xiao. She framed them for killing her baby girl and practising black magic.

The history book pointed to Wu Zetian killing her own flesh and blood for the purpose of framing Empress Wang.

She ordered the execution of the Empress Wang and Consort Xiao by beating them a hundred times and chopping off their hands and legs before soaking them in wine. Both ladies suffered greatly before death. Consort Xiao vowed to come back as a cat to haunt Wu Zetian.

For the rest of her lives, she had a morbid fear of cat.

Empress Wu Zetian became the invisible ruling power from the year 660 onwards. She took steps to kill all the officers who opposed her and to consolidate her ruling power. Whenever Emperor Tang Gaozong held court, Empress Wu would sit behind the curtain and command him to act.

After the death of Emperor Tang Gaozhong, Empress Wu continued to hold actual ruling power behind all the puppet emperors.

In the year 690, she dethroned the puppet emperor, declared herself as Sacred and Divine Empress Regnant and founded her own Dynasty.

Was she a good Emperor?

There was no doubt that Empress Wu was a very formidable woman. Much as she was feared and hated by her enemies, historians admitted that she was a very capable and far sighted ruler.

During her reign, she improved on the imperial examination so as to recognise talents. She took the trouble to preside over the examinations, and conducted oral examinations of scholars who had passed a few rounds of examinations. She had the ability to recognise talent and managed talent. The family background of the scholars did not matter, what really matter was the potential.

On the same note, once she discovered incompetency among the court officials, she would take action to remove them from office.

Empress Wu exercised good judgments in her ruling, so much so that nobody can fault her on her policy making skills. She improved on the agricultural and commercial development of the country. She settled the border dispute and brought peace to the people living near the border.

Under her rulership, the population increased at an average rate of 9.1%. People enjoyed peace and prosperity. The court was full of talented officers serving the ordinary people. She passed away in 705, living beyond 80 years old.

Empress Wu's achievement testified to her intelligent and beauty. She was able to understand the big picture and made strategic plans. She did not have anyone to help her since her father passed away when she was very young. She did not even have a mentor to guide her. Since she was the first and only female Emperor, she had no one to model after.

Wu Zetian was the only female emperor in the Chinese feudal dynasties spanning more than 4,000 years. With exceptional wisdom and great talent, she was a cruel and merciless woman, who would reach her goals by fair means or foul. Nevertheless, she made great political achievements. Even today, movies and TV plays featuring her life are drawing great attention and research interest.

When I looked down at my shoes, this time, I was amazed. I freaked out!

I felt terrified!

I was wearing tiny shoes, size two, or zero, like baby shoes, or doll's shoes.

I had lotus blossom feet!

That's a pretty way of describing feet that had been broken on purpose and bound for decades, from childhood, and had never grown normally.

The bones of children are softer, break more easily, and heal faster, they say.

The goal was to have pretty little feet.

The goal was to marry money. Ad with bound and broken feet, I could not run away from my husband, or even walke.

They liked that!

He had to carry me from the bedroom to the kitchen.

I wanted to kill him.

But how? I could barely stand up!

He looked like a different person, or had a different aura, the second time I saw him in Dalain in 690. He looked happy and he looked at me without staring or glaring.

He started to walk toward me and he was going to say something, obviously, but he was interrupted by a knock on the door, again, so he turned on his heel and he was gone.

A woaman came in as he went out.

Who was this woman with enormous feet?

I started at her shoes until I realized her feet were normal, not bound, like mine, and stuffed into doll's shoes.

She looked happy to see me.

Why cry? she said.

It was like talking to my daughter, except she didn't ask me to do anything.

She wanted to tell me a lot of things.

I just got back from acupuncture, she said quickly, and I have some new herbs to take. The doctor stuck a lot of pins in me this time and burned herbs at the same time. When he uses his fingers like needles, he hurt murt so much I dropped to my knees.

She went on and on about Traditional Chinese Medicine.

Men! she said. I could kill all of them.

Sometimes, she added.

Why don't we ....

I started to say something but she cut me off.

"The emperor got rid of another man today, she said excitedly. That makes one for every day this week!"

Why cry? my daughter said.

I had to look away, out a window.

Outside, I saw a beautiful, natural world: blue skies, blue water in a round bay with serrated hills behind it. Apparently we lived in a house on a hill by a big bay, some huge body of water.

As I started at the water, which looked wide enough to be a sea, it turned yllow.

It was be a trick of the sunlight, I thought, the light shining on the water in a different way, or maybe there was something in the water.

I could not speak, I was so upset.

I pointed to the door and my daughter walked away.

I imagined waling beside the bay I could see from my window. I walked backwards, in my imagination, visualizing escaping from that place, backing away into the future.

The beach went on forever but I didn't feel like walking or putting my feet in the water or doing anything except flying from that time back to the here and now that I knew, so it was April 11, 2014, once again.

Time travel is dangerous, I decided. I did not want to do it again. Ever.

Suddenly, everything in my life in 2014 looked simple, easy, positive, and smart.

Going back in time and finding myself in the body and mind of a woman was not something I wanted to do again, ever, in this or any other lifetime. But I wanted to find out more about that tall man who talked about law or business or politics in languages I could not understand.

For a white man to become a Chinese woman, to transform from a privileged member of the patriarchy into a woman in a society where there was an even greater loevl of status for men was so shocking I just wanted to get the hell out of there.

However,   after I reassured myself, made sure I could come back to the future, and I wasn't stuck in that time, I had a strong desire to go back and experience more with that man in that place.

Who was he? And why did I want to kill him?

And what about the other women? Did they feel the same way as me?

What was my name? What was my city's name? What was my husband's problem?

I had to go back.

You're my husband, I said flatly.

He glared at me.

You're my wife, he said.

My heart sank all the way down to my broken feet.

Right down to the bottom of the soles of my little shoes.

How did anybody walk, wearing such tiny shoes, with re-broken feet?

I felt like running, so I took a step, to see what I could do.

A pain shot up my leg from the bottom of my feet through all twelve meridians and stayed in my brain. I had a huge migraine headache and I hurt all over.

I must have passed out after my first step in that life because I don't recall falling or being scooped up but I woke up to find I was in the arms of the tall man.

Going somewhere? he said.

To bed, I said meekly.

He stared or glared. I looked away.

There was a knock at the door at the moment he dropped e on a hard bed, and he hurried off.

I listened hard and half-heard him speaking to another man. He spoke a language I did not understand, or a dialect so different that it sounded like another tongue.

The men talked about legal matters laws, and money.

The man who said he was my husband closed the door so I could not hear. As soon as the door slammed, I started to sob.

I cried for a long time. My feet hurt, my head hurt, my heart hurt. My brain felt as though it was getting zapped by little bolts of lightning.

I cursed the tall man and wished evil things on him: I hoped he was reincarnated as a woman with bound and broken feet, with sore feet and legs, with pain that shot through his meridians and hit his brain like an electrical storm.

I wished I was a man.

But I swore I would be a better man than him.

If I was a man and he was a woman and we met again, sometime in the future ....

What would I do?

Would I recognize him?

Or her?

What kind of a woman would he be.

Were all women like me? I wondered. Did I have sisters, a mother, mother-in-law, grandmothers, girlfriends, daughters?

I felt a strong desire to gather them all together or talk to them all somehow. If only there was some way to contact other women, one at a time or in groups, or as one big group.

How many women were there where I lived?

Where did we live?

What did I know about my city, my country, the world and all the women in it?

Thinking in Chinese was quite different, I discovered. The precision of the English language was replaced by beautiful characters symbolizing concepts.

could I use them to communicate with other women? To find out if they felt the same way as me?

A little girl walked into my room. She looked just like me, or a combination of the all man and me.

It's time to bind my feet, she said.

I cried.

Chapter 8. A Future Life: Chinese Women Will Take Over The World

I looked down at my feet and an odd thought popped into my head: Why did I wear high heels today?

Why did I ever wear high heels? They were hard to walk in, slowed me down, and hurt my feet!

I saw a callous by my little toe and had a flashback to the time I had bound feet.

Instead of getting angry, I smiled remembering many of my past lives, what I learned and what it had to do with my life in the present moment, the here and now, which was ..... When?

I focused on my breathing as I looked at my wrist-top computer. It said it was 9:38 in the morning in Dalian, China, on April 23, 2085, and it was foggy, 23 degrees, going up to 25, and my Google stocks, left to me by my former self, were going through the glass ceiling!

So, many of my fears, and the fears of my era, turned out to be nightmares that did not come true.

The warnings about global warming, rising oceans, melting glaciers, the Arctic melting, tsunamis, pandemics, bird flu, swine flu, super-sizing, jihads, terrorists, the Middle East, religious fundamentalists, the U.K. and the U.S.A. versus the old U.SSR, the European Union versus Africa, China versus Japan, Quebec versus Canada, oil pipelines, tar sands, heavy metal rock bands .... You know, we didn't start the fire, as the American singer/songwriter Billy Joel said a long time ago: the world's been burning since the world's been turning .....

Air pollution, oil addiction, drugs in American and europe, South America civil wars, I can't take it any more!

It's 2014, now, so it's two years after the date many people said would be the end of the world.

The same thing happened at the turn of the century. I wrote a book about it called Preparing For The Millennium. The Y2K Bug got a lot of attention at that time. It was predicted that computers all over the world would fail, along with the banking, health, transportation, and all other systems controlled by them.

I got on the bandwagon for Global Warming early but, after everybody else got on board, I jumped off.

Don't get me wrong! I'm still enormously concerned about wild weather on our planet, caused by pollution created by people.
Canada had a wicked winter this year, but I missed it by moving to China.

There are many climate refugees already and many people have lost their lives due to weather events connected to global warming.

The rest of us carry on like we are in a play by Samuel Becket. I can't go on! we say. But then we carry on.

The future predicted by John Wyndham in The Chrysalids is not likely to come true.

My new Age guru says a golden age is coming, in the not too distant future, for select groups.

My wrist told me I had an early morning meeting, a breakfast meeting, a brunch meeting, a lunch meeting, a meeting at tea time, a supper meeting, a meeting over drinks after dinner, and then a party, just like yesterday and tomorrow, and it showed I had several e-mails as well as Facebook messages, plus texts and phone calls to return.

One of the messages was from Korea. It said, Since the reunification, the area formerly known as North Korea, the darkest part of the planet, in terms of electric lights, between China and Russia, was a great place to invest as the real estate boom was fantastic. Where else could you find rural property in the hills, by the sea, with four seasons, that wasn't already over-developed, over-used, and over-priced?

Another message made fun of global warming, comparing it to Y2K and 2012, and made reference to the simple trick that had stabilized temperatures around the world, which prevented the flooding of coastlines and stopped the trend toward wilder and wilder weather. Apparently an idea that a Canadian writer came up with, that called for the creation of fake icebergs, made out of recycled plastic from the Pacific Ocean, filled the Arctic Ocean with reflective surfaces as well as places for polar bears to play. A lot of light was reflected back into space, the water cooled, the ice returned, the big white bears didn't have to swim so much, and it was all good, as they used to say around the turn of the century.

My wrist also had the details of my travel itinerary for the upcoming Labor Day Holiday, which was one week at the start of May. I would be traveling by train from Dalian to Bejing to Shanghai to Hong Kong and then to the big island that had called itself Taiwan, up to our new colony, formerly known as Japan, and then to Vladivostock, where I took the train across Korea, back to Dalian. It was a counter-clockwise circle, I noticed, so I had my online personal assistant reverse everything.

During my week-long vacation, I had a big decision to make, according to my daily planner. In bold letters, it said, Get back to the UN re: new job.

I looked out the window and recognized the view: I was in a new building overlooking Kaifaqu and the Yellow Sea, so I had to be on one of the Black Mountains. If memory served, it looked as though I was on the biggest hill in the area, called Big Black, or Big Monk Mountain, or Grand Monk, back in the day, when the same area was occupied by China after Russia after Japan after the Mongols.

In a flash, I realized why I was born where I was in the 1950s, in my last life: Because I grew up in a house that was right behind a big old barn of an arena used as a hockey rink, I had a great opportunity to play the national game, in Canada, and hockey had taught me how to be a manly man. My father and his father were both war heroes whose lives were ruined by World War One and Two. The little town where my father was forced to settle in, after the war, because he had TB, from clearing out Nazi concentration camps at the end of his war, was the home of the Northern Book House, the number one distribution centre for communist propaganda from the Soviet Union, and the location of the Bethune

House, where Dr. Norman Bethune was born, and it was close to the towns that gave the world Bobby Orr, the best hockey player in history, and Stephen Leacock, a well-known humorist and writer in the early days of Canadian Literature. I realized that I picked my parents and that place so I would get a great education in what it meant to be a man.

My mother's father was a great role model and so was my main literary mentor, W.O. Mitchell. I had hockey coaches and elementary school teachers, English teachers in high school and Writing teachers at university, as well as a Buddhist monk who was a Zen master, to give me great examples of what kind of man I could be.

After going to Beijing University and working at the Bethune International Peace Hospital, getting a great education and experience as in integrated medicine, combining the best of the East and the West, with Traditional Chinese Medicine plus Ayervedic medicine from India, as well as the latest research and technology from Europe and North America, I had a desire to move on from the medical field and get in touch with my spiritual side. I did yoga in the early morning, qigung after meditation, and I got a lot of writing done at the same time.

After my first few books were published and won some prizes after being on the best-seller lists in China and the U.S.A., as well as various countries in Europe, plus Canada and the Commonwealth countries, I got invited to travel around the world on a book tour, to promote the books, so I did talk shows everywhere and became quite famous. After a few non-fiction books, I thought I'd try my hand at a novel.

My first novel turned into a series of novels that proved to be even more popular than my non-fiction, even though I was writing about the same things: healing, combining the best of the East and the West, and the ancient with the latest in medicine, with some romance added in there to make the story a little juicier. My fiction was marketed as Y.A. and teenagers around the world gobbled it up, for some reason. My publisher said it was because it was so optimistic about the future and so full of love. Apparently that's what kids nowadays are interested in: love and the future.

It makes sense: They ARE the future!

The next thing you know, one of my books was bought by Hollywood and turned into a movie, as a co-production with a company in China, and then I was very famous.

Academic awards and other honours followed, so, before too long, as well as signing M.D. after my name, I could add Ph.d., a few times, and Rev., before. When I was introduced, before giving a speech, they called me Reverened Doctor ....

Political appointments followed that, but I didn't agree to take any positions that were just for show, I took on jobs that allowed me to actually do things. I always enjoyed getting things done. And that's how I got to the U.N., in N.Y.C..

And once I was at the NYC UN, I started a program to move the United Nations out of the old building in the U.S.A. and into a new building in China.

It felt like the right time to make the move, since the age of the American Empire was definitely over and China was leading the world.

In days of old, when knights were bold, in Europe, China led Asia, when we thought Asia was the whole world, but now China really was leading the whole world.

And it was Chinese women who were at the helm, this time, just like in the old days of Emperor Wu, when China was a young country.

So maybe it was only natural that a high profile, highly educated, accomplished and honoured woman from China would become the Secretary General of the U.N. when it opened its doors in China.

My choice of location for the UN's new HQ caused some controversy in China, as the capital of the country and the big cities all thought the honour should go to them, but I wanted it to be in the city I considered to be the capital of the New China, which just happened to be the city I came from, where I grew up and went to school, before I went to school in Beijing and went to work in Shizhaungziez. Besides, there was an undeveloped wilderness area on the big old mountain in the free trade zone of Dalian. Yes, Grand Monk Mountain in the Kaifaqu area became the home of the new UN. We picked up a property close to an ancient Taoist temple compound called "Dragon Spits On Lotus".

Critics said the UN should have a higher profile location, so we took over the front face of the mountain and turned it into a huge billboard by adding decorative waterfalls that spelled out U and N.

They were the biggest waterfalls in Asia, so they became quite a tourist attraction, and they were shown on TV news shows every day so Dalian and the Grand Monk Mountain were famous all over the world.

life expectancy in 2200 will be around 100 for developed countries and the world population will be about 8.5 billion.

an ongoing confrontation between an increasingly powerful Mexico and the United States will be taking place.[dubious – discuss] Mexico will be an economically and militarily powerful country capable of challenging the United States, while a Mexican majority in southern regions of the United States will have made them a de facto extension of Mexico, with increasing secessionist sentiment. Both countries will be competing for dominance over North America, which will remain the international centre of gravity throughout the next few centuries.

By 2100, 12% (about 1250) of the bird species existing at the beginning of the 21st century are expected to be extinct or threatened with extinction.

By 2100, Emperor Penguins could be pushed to the brink of extinction due to global climate change, according to a Woods Hole Oceanographic Institution study from January 2009. The study applied mathematical models to predict how the loss of sea ice from climate warming would affect an Antarctica colony of Emperor Penguins, and they forecast a decline of 87% in the colony's population by the end of the century.

ChinaCan

If on a winter's night a traveller hears a screaming come across the sky, he might look up and see his own life passing by. It could be a drone from some foreign country, operating like a spy in years gone by.

Welcome to the future, as Brad Paisley, the American country singer says.

Margaret Atwood predicted a flood and a future full of genetic hybrids like a cross between a skunk and a raccoon in a trilogy of novels she wrote in her seventies and published in the 2010s when global warming was the biggest issue on the planet Earth. Of course, it was not the end of the world as we knew it, it just looked and felt that way to people obsessed with the environment. Politics was something else.

Poverty was the issue, not pollution. And the battle between communism and democracy was ending. First, capitalism destroyed communism in the U.S.S.R. and then capitalism destroyed democracy in the U.S.A. With the two superpowers knocked down, knocked out, it was time for a former superpower to make a comeback, after being down and out, and lead the world to its new birth, as Norman Bethune once said.

When China took over Canada, or the two countries merged, to become ChinaCan, there was no war, no take-over, no violence or bloodshed, no conflict. It was the kind of battle Canada was famous for: it featured compromise and peace-keeping.

True, Canada had recently and formerly pursued a peculiar battle plan, lying low for a century or two and then attacking Libya. After 150 years of helping the United Nations keep peace, I thought Canada should have snuck up on Turkey, taken it over, renamed it Chicken. Instead, Canada followed the lead of the superpower next door and fought Moslem nations for oil, even though Canada already half the world's oil, in the tarsands of Alberta. But Canada sold the tarsands to China.

Canada and China getting together to form the new superpower called ChinaCan was incredibly logical and appeared obvious, after it happened. On the one hand, there was a big country with 1.3 billion people and on the other hand there was a bigger country with incredible natural resources. Why not put the two together and save the world that was almost destroyed by the U.S.A. and the U.S.S.R. during the Cold War, which led to Global Warming?!

Like Israel taking over Palestine at the end of World War Two, after the Holocaust, China took over Canada not with military might but a checque-book. China already owned the U.S.A., in a sense, as it held trillions of dollars worth of the American national debt. Canada, with its mixed economy, part capitalist and part socialist, was a better money manager, but its economy was closely tied to the economy of the enormous country to the south. It was like a mouse sleeping next to an elephant, a famous Canadian said, but when the elephant went bankrupt, what was the mouse to do? Canada welcomed Chinese investment and countless Canadian teachers were glad to get jobs in China, teaching English, to help the Chinese take over their country.

Close to the heart of all that action was a man named Norman Bethune and a small town in Canada called Bethune, as Mao Zhe Dong, the leader of the revolution that led China out of poverty and through the industrial era to the consumer society, had praised the Canadian doctor for his selfless devotion to the cause and connected the two countries forever. Canadians saw Bethune differently than the Chinese, but that's another story. They were happy to embrace the controversial doctor if it meant Canada would rise up with China instead of going down with the U.S.A.

Our story begins in 2023, a decade after that unlucky year, 2013, which was the year after millions of New Agers said the world would end, and when most of the world was worried about Global Warming. There were lots of predictions about global catastrophe, especially floods with tsunamis, and the New Agers revised their predictions, saying it would be the end of the world for many but the start of a Golden New Age for a select number of highly evolved or enlightened people. It turned out to be far simpler than that: Low-lying coastal areas in or on the oceans were flooded, those who stayed were lost, and the weather refugees who made it to higher ground survived. That was it.

The Arctic melted but that meant another ocean could be criss-crossed and explored, opening up trade routes and things to trade for. Many southerners were making a lot of noise about saving the Arctic. But Global Warming was a hard sell in northern nations.

"What? It's getting a little warmer? Bring it on!" they said.

Tell someone in North Bay or Northern Ontario, or Cold Lake or anywhere in Northern Alberta that the winters are going to be a bit warmer and see how upset they get.

They will try to kiss you.

The same was true in Siberia, of course.

Even Northern China.

Southern China was used to the heat, so a few degrees more did not make them freak out. The new spiritual leader was not the Dalai Lama or the Pope or any of the high profile religious leaders of the turn of the century or the early years of the new millennium. The new spiritual leader was a Vietnamese-Canadian guy who created a Zen retreat in the Far East of Ontario called The Zen Forest. He was called The One Who Teaches Zen. Since I was born in 1955, I will likely die around 2055, so I could be reborn shortly after that, which means I could be twenty years old in 2075.

I will be a Chinese woman, going to The Bethune International Peace University, studying integrative medicine, combining Traditional Chinese Medicine with Western Medicine, majoring in qigun and spiritual healing.

My mother wanted me to be a doctor or a minister but I grew up in a house that was right behind a hockey arena and that big old barn of a building inspired me to become a novice in the game that is Canada's national religion, so I spent a decade playing hockey, but then I got back on track, going to university and going on a great journey to learn all about writing and art, then spirituality and healing.

Bethune died in Tangxian county, Baoding, Hebei province. To commemorate him as a great international fighter, a wartime local hospital was named Bethune International

Peace Hospital, and it still operates, in Shijiazhuang, capital of Hebei. Bethune is buried at the North China Military Martyrs Cemetery in Shijiazhuang.

Dr Bethune, a thoracic surgeon and member of the Canadian Communist Party, led a medical team to save injured soldiers in China during the War of Resistance against Japanese Aggression (1937-45).

The Bethune International Peace Hospital is located south of Beijing in the city of Shijiazhuang. For patients arriving by plane in Beijing, the drive to Shijiazhuang may take 4-5 hours depending on traffic. While most patients find it easier to arrive in Beijing, it is possible, depending upon departure city, to connect straight to Shijiazhuang. Because of Beijing's proximity, many patients choose to visit Beijing before, during, or after treatment and see such sights as the Great Wall, Forbidden City, and the Olympic complex.

The hospital has 52 departments, 84 professional and technical staff of more than 1,500 employees, including 238 higher-level experts. The hospital has added an additional 2,000 beds. During the year the hospital has 77 million annual outpatient visits and does over 6 billion in business.

I went from high school to Beijing University and then to the Bethune International Peace Hospital. After working for a while as a doctor in China and the U.S.A., as well as Canada and India, I wrote several books that became big bestsellers, won the Nobel Prizes for Peace, Literature, and Healing, went on a world tour to promote peace love and harmony through making love like a Taoist, and then was appointed Secretary General of the United Nations.

I met a man who reminded me of me in a past life but was also like my Zen master, my main mentor as a writer, my grandfather, but was actually the reincarnation of several woman I had known and loved in my last life.

Talk about Rumi reborn!

We do not heal the past by dwelling there, Marianne Williamson said, we heal the past by living fully in the present. Marianne Williamson is a spiritual teacher, author and lecturer. She has published ten books, including four New York Times #1 bestsellers.

But that's not the point, here. We heal the present by doing past life work and that is something that helps us live fully in the present.

The man and the woman who make the journey up the mountain to the Dragon Spitting On Lotus Temple discover how to use the chakras, the meridians, chi, and love for health and happiness, energy and longevity, peace and love, understanding and compassion, empathy and harmony. They forge a plan to spend the rest of their lives together.

After that moment of profound revelation, the man realized he was not with a woman, listening to a talking dragon. He was alone while meditating and hearing a voice that was, in reality, his own. He went to the mountain looking for a Taoist master and realized that he was a Zen master, Reiki master, and energy healer with a diploma in spiritual healing, so, of course, he was, in fact, a Taoist master.

About the author ....

Canadian author Martin Avery, now living in China, wrote 100 books set in the West and is now working on 100 books set in the East.

A short list of some related books by the same author

1. Secrets of Love, Health, and Wealth, With Grace And Ease and Perfect Timing
2. Simple Simon's Guide To Zen Meditation
3. Zen Forest Meditations
4. Wake Up Here And Now: How To Recover Your Life Before It's Over
5. How To Die Laughing
6. Eat More, Pray More, Love More
7. 2012 O.M
8. 2035 O.M
9. The Woman Who Woke Up In The Zen Forest
10. Healing 2012 To 2035

Zen books
1. Zen Forest: True Nature
2. Zen Is Not In Books!
3. The Zen Forest A To Z
4. Zen Forest Haiku
6. Zen Power Hour
7. Zen Forest Meditations
8. A Zen Forest In Canada
9. Zen Writing
10, A Short-Cut To Enlightenment

12. Zen Forest Visitor's Guide

13. Santa Claus And The Laughing Buddha

14. The Woman Who Woke Up In The Zen Forest

15. Brigit's Bardot

16, The Way Of The Quiet Canadian Warrior

17. Long Quiet Canadian Highway

The Great Wall Of China Books Series

1. From Bethune's Birthplace To The People's Republic Of China (memoir)

2. Swimming To China (poetry)

3. Mo Yan And Me (short novel)

4. Far Away, Dalian, Far Away (travel)

5. A Trip Around Lake Muskoka With Norman Bethune (short novel)

6. In Love And War

7. Chinese Kisses (poetry)

8. My Chinese Metamorphosis (poetry)

9. Hockey Night In China (non-fiction)

10. An Intro To Acupuncture And TCM (non-fiction)

11. Norman Bethune's Tears Cure Cancer (novel)

12. Bethune Returns To China (novel)

13. Bethune's Time (novel)

14. The Bethune Trilogy: A Trip Around Lake Muskoka With Norman Bethune, Bethune's Tears Cure Cancer, Bethune Returns To China

15. Good News From China (found poetry)

16. Suzanne Takes You Down (novel)

17. The Woman Who Was Picked Up By A Monk (poetry)

18. Bethune Buttons (poetry)

19. Dear China: Love Letter Poems

www.ingramcontent.com/pod-product-compliance
Lightning Source LLC
Chambersburg PA
CBHW020628130626
46552CB00003B/1130